Italian Writers

BIRD OF
PARADISE

Costanzo Costantini

BIRD OF PARADISE

Translated from the Italian by
Anne Milano Appel

GREMESE

Everyone knows that life isn't worth living[1]
Albert Camus, *The Stranger*

*Judging whether life is or is not
worth living amounts to answering
the fundamental question of philosophy.[2]*
Albert Camus, *The Myth of Sisyphus*

Original title:
L'uccello del paradiso

Cover:
apostoli & maggi – Rome

Phototypesetting and Photoprinting:
Graphic Art 6 s.r.l. – Rome
E-mail: dva@uni.net

Press:
C.S.R. – Rome

GREMESE
1st Edition © 2000
E.G.E. s.r.l. – Rome

*All rights reserved. No part of this publication may be repro-
duced, recorded or transmitted in any form or by any
means without the prior written permission of the Publisher.*

ISBN 88-7301-403-8

THE MYTH OF SISYPHUS

I searched for Marta all night long.

I phoned all of her friends, male and female.

I made the rounds of the cafes, discotheques and restaurants.

I went to the Vice Squad and the Emergency Rooms at the hospitals.

I even went to the Tiber.

I walked along the embankment in one direction and then the other, from Cavour bridge to Mazzini bridge and vice versa, among the whores, the transvestites, the derelicts and the would be suicides. In the sections where structures kept me from walking along the river, I watched its flow from the bridges. From time to time I seemed to make out a head, a back. They were pulled up by the current and then sucked back under by it. It was impossible to tell if they belonged to men or women, old or young. Only a madman would think he could identify a body from that distance in those dark, filthy depths, that shadowy atmosphere. After walking back and forth for a long time, I convinced myself that Marta's body wasn't there and I abandoned the search.

Now I am in Piazza di Spagna, at the corner of Via dei Condotti.

The clock in the piazza reads four o'clock.

It is the only thing moving in the scene which is displayed before me.

If I stare at it, I can catch the movement of the hands, but the whiteness of the disk blinds me.

The lights are all out, even those on the roof of the Hassler.

Only the light of the Quirinale tower is lit, but it looks like the flame of a cemetery plot suspended in the air.

The profile of the church of Trinità dei Monti is just barely outlined in the purple light of the coming dawn.

"Let her go to hell!" I tell myself, starting to go up to the house to go to bed. But instead of going toward the door of the building in which I live, I set out as though instinctively, without wanting to, in the direction of Via del Babuino, and turn into Via dei Greci. I pass a prostitute with no clients, who assumes an ungainly, monstrous appearance in the deserted street. Then, near the silverware shop, the usual encounter with the old man – the demoniacal old man with the deformed face and the eyes of a mole – who rummages in the trash bin of the nearby restaurant, cheating the stray cats in the neighborhood. At one time he used to look at me askance, full of venom. Now he doesn't turn around anymore. Perhaps he despises me. I am the only witness to his degradation.

I move on hardly noticing, and reach the door marked number 75.

I climb the stairs, without any apparent haste, until I reach the seventh floor.

I open the door, cautiously.

The stereo is turned up full volume to a Gainsbourg recording, there are clothes thrown on the floor, dirty dishes, broken glasses, overflowing ashtrays...

I look into the bedroom: Marta is wheezing faintly, a nearly imperceptible wince on her contracted face, her legs spread apart.

I lift her from the bed and shake her, but there is no sign of a reaction.

I call 113.

Rome is an Indian city, a Calcutta on the Tiber.

I've been waiting for over half an hour.

I am reminded of my neighbor, who, when his wife was dying, was unable to find an ambulance the entire night.

My senses have expanded.

The slightest noise makes me jump.

I feel overcome by an excessive agitation that borders on rage, a power and impotence never before experienced.

Finally the ambulance arrives.

"We're here" a deep voice announces on the intercom.

Exactly forty-five minutes have gone by.

"In forty-five minutes anyone could die, even a person who still had the will to live" I think.

Yet the voice on the telephone had told me:

"We'll be there immediately".

I go down to escort them upstairs.

Two uninterested looking guys appear before me.

"What floor?" they ask.

I show them the way up.

We climb the stairs without speaking.

Marta is wheezing ever more faintly.

They take her, carry her down, put her in the van, and arrange her on the bed. One of the two goes up front to drive, the other sits next to her to support her. He never looks at her face, but from time to time he can't resist a furtive glance at her legs, each time a brusque jolt of the ambulance causes her dressing gown to open.

Luckily the hospital is nearby.

We don't exchange a single word along the way. Nor do we say goodbye when they go off to pick up another person on his deathbed, after having dropped off Marta.

Two nurses move Marta into a room.

I start to follow them but one of them says to me:

"You can't come in".

I sit on a bench, light a cigarette, and wait.
I am alone. No voices. I don't know what is going on.

A doctor appears, in pajamas and slippers; he looks
around, he rubs his eyes, he comes up to me:
"You're the husband?"
"No".
"A relative?"
"No".
"What is your relationship to her?"
"I'm a friend".
"Do you know her well?"
"I think so".
"Is she a tense person?"
"No more than any of us".
"But before taking the barbiturates, was she stressed out?"
"I wouldn't say so".
He shakes his head and goes away.

I am tempted to take it as a favorable sign. He wasted
valuable time asking me foolish questions. But I have no
faith in logic.
I get up, light another cigarette, and begin to pace back
and forth along the corridor.

A door opens suddenly.
It is not the room where the two nurses took Marta.
A man about twenty-five years old comes out, no jacket,
wrinkled white shirt, a coarse, puffy face, but acting like
God Almighty. He makes a disdainful gesture indicating that
I should follow him.
The following words are written on a brass plate:
"Police Office".
He invites me to come in and sit down, looking at me sus-
piciously while taking his place behind the desk.
"Do you have identification?"

"My identification card". I hand it to him.

"What do you do?"

"I have a degree in Humanities".

"Do you teach?"

"No".

"Are you a writer like Moravia, Pasolini?"

"I write mysteries. Now I'm going to write one with you as the protagonist. You'll become the new Maigret".

"Don't be funny. Tell me: What is your relationship with Ms. Cohen?"

"She's a friend".

"You mean your lover?"

"If you say so".

"Have you been seeing her for a long time?"

"Long enough".

"How long?"

"Several months".

"When did she try to kill herself?"

"Tonight".

"At what time?"

"I couldn't tell you exactly".

"Why?"

"Because I wasn't with her".

"Where did she take the barbiturates?"

"In her apartment, on Via dei Greci 75".

"But you were the one who came to her assistance: how did you know she needed help?"

"Since she didn't answer my phone calls, and since I couldn't find her anywhere, I decided to go and wait for her outside the house: sooner or later she would come back. I didn't think I would find her there".

"You had the keys?"

"I'm not a housebreaker".

He gives me an ironic smile as if to say: "I'm not too sure".

"Why did she try to kill herself?"

"I don't know".

"Was she drunk?"

"I don't know".

"Was she drugged?"

"I don't know".

"Do you take drugs?"

"I should, to tolerate people like you".

"Even funnier".

"Thank you".

"Did you have an argument?"

"No".

"Then why didn't she want you to find her?"

"Probably she didn't answer the telephone or the intercom because she had already taken the barbiturates".

"How many did she take?"

"There was an empty tube on the bed, but I don't know how many were in there. You can ask the doctors, if you really want to know".

He shakes his head, with a mocking grin... Then he tries to find a more comfortable position, making the chair squeak, and begins to type: "Andrea Boldini came to the aid of Marta Cohen..."

He then makes me sign the report and dismisses me abruptly.

"Thank you" I say to him while leaving the room, but I think to myself "you big shit".

I go back to sitting on the bench.

I still don't know anything about Marta's condition.

"If things were to go badly, they would tell me" I think. But logical as it may be, the thought does not ease my apprehension.

The doctor from before comes out again:

"Ms. Cohen is sleeping. If there are no complications in the following hours, she'll be out of danger. You can come back tomorrow morning, or rather this morning, at noon.

Toward noon, there I am back at the hospital.

Marta is out of danger; she smiles gently at me.

Another doctor tells me:

"She made it. She has a very strong heart. Tomorrow we'll make a decision".

I don't know what decision he is referring to, but I refrain from asking him to explain. I don't want to lose the sense of relief that his words have given me.

I stay with Marta until the nurses order me to leave.

The babel of the Holy Year is at its peak; Rome is about to explode.

But I feel happy.

The following morning, at noon, I return to the hospital.

Marta is beginning to regain her self-awareness, and cannot hide a vague sense of guilt. She would like to leave the hospital in order to forget.

"I'll take you away soon" I tell her.

But the doctor who had told me she was out of danger intervenes:

"It's a complicated case" he tells me.

"What's complicated about it?"

"We don't know if it's appropriate to release Ms. Cohen. It's a question of accountability. In any case, it's not up to me to decide. Talk to the psychiatrist".

The psychiatrist is a woman in her thirties.

Tall, sturdy, sure of herself.

The type who thinks "I know all about the mysteries of the human soul".

"Are you the one who came to Ms. Cohen's assistance and accompanied her here?" she asks, looking at me disdainfully as though it were my fault that Marta filled herself with barbiturates.

"Yes".

"Ms. Cohen cannot be released" she tells me with a peremptory tone.

"Excuse me, why not?"

"She has a dangerous tendency toward self-destruction. This is the third time she's tried to kill herself. We have to keep her here to explore her personality more thoroughly, identify her deep impulses, and prescribe treatment. If we don't, the next time she will kill herself for real".

"Why do you think she will kill herself for real?"

"Because she has no will to live".

"Excuse me, but if we had to detain all those who have no will to live or lock them up in hospitals, very few would remain outside".

"And you wouldn't be among them".

"Maybe, but I would never want to be treated by you".

"You'd have to be admitted in any case".

"A scientist like you should know that the only serious question is whether life is or is not worth living, as Camus says in the *Myth of Sisyphus*".

"Look, I can't waste my time with you, you're still back in high school".

"But I do know it's up to Ms. Cohen to decide what she wants to do with herself".

"I hope Ms. Cohen doesn't ask for your help".

"I'll see to it that she doesn't ask for yours, you can be sure of it".

"I understand" she says, with an ironic smile.

"I'm glad" I reply, but I would like to say: "You think you understand everything, you prick of a super woman".

"Go ahead and kill yourself with your friend, if that's what you want to do" she adds sarcastically.

"I will" I reply, but I think "first I'd like to kill you".

"If you want to take her away, Ms. Cohen must first give us her written assurance that she is leaving the hospital of her own free will".

"Go ahead and ask Ms. Cohen".

The psychiatrist asks Ms. Cohen if she wants to be released.
"Yes" Marta answers without hesitation.
"Sign here" the psychiatrist says, handing her a sheet of paper which is ready and waiting.
Marta signs it.
"Good luck, Ms. Cohen" the psychiatrist tells her, adding in a tone that is somewhere between ironic and sarcastic: "I hope I don't see you again too soon".
"Thank you, you're very kind" I say, but I think to myself "we hope we don't see you ever again".

Marta goes into the ward to get dressed, says goodbye to the women who are staying behind, and we leave.

The sky is a radiant blue.
Marta walks as though in a trance. Beneath the sun's rays, the waxen pallor of her face, with that long slim body, gives her a ghostly air.

"I'm famished" she says, as we walk along Via del Corso, leaving the hospital of San Giacomo behind us.

We go into the first restaurant we come to.

Without waiting for the waiter to show us to a table, Marta fills a plate with various items from the antipasto bar, sets it down on the first free table, sits down and begins to eat.
I take some antipasto as well, and ask for a bottle of wine.
"To you" I say, raising my glass in a toast.
She drinks almost the entire glass in one gulp, and finishes the antipasto.
"I'm still hungry" she says, drawing my attention to her empty plate with a glance.
"What would you like?" I ask her. But without answering, she gets up and fills another plate.

She frees her right foot and slips it between my legs...

"Come with me" she says, getting up and leading me toward the bathroom.

She pulls up her skirt, pulls down her panties, frantically...

"Let's go" she says.
I pay the bill and we leave.

We make the trip from Via del Corso to Via dei Greci 75 breathlessly, she in front, me behind.

She opens the front door urgently.

After climbing six or seven steps she stops, sits down, and spreads her legs, pulling down her panties and torn stockings...

She gets up and we continue climbing the stairs.

As soon as we're in the house, she pushes me onto the bed and falls upon me with savage heat.

I remain on the bed, stunned.

After a while I feel her panting breath on my face, the sweaty scent of her body next to mine.

AN *AMOUR FOU*

I met Marta Cohen at Sandro Spigai's studio on Via Margutta, the artists' street in Rome, where even Picasso had a studio at one time.

Sandro Spigai is an abstract expressionist painter, who began his artistic career in New York. To be precise, he's more of an expressionist, or neo-expressionist, than an abstract artist. His scenes of New York are very beautiful: the great metropolis emanates from them through a dense, thick substance, an infernal energy, which is at the same time luminous and transparent, and yet it appears always about to collapse, to implode, as though from an endogenous earthquake. His paintings are sought by Italian and foreign museums, but that does not faze him in the least; he accepts it with supreme indifference. He has not the slightest interest in success, nor in money. He paints out of inertia, just as he lives by inertia. Every six months he tries to kill himself; and he survives the failed suicide by telling all of his friends how and why he didn't die. It is not by chance that the painters he loves the most are Rothko and Gorky, both suicides. In addition, he thinks that others are obligated to compensate him for the misfortune of being on earth. He considers existence to be a sentence which only suicide can bring to an end.

It is through Sandro Spigai that I came to know Judith Friedman and her friend, Alfred Miller, both New Yorkers. Alfred was working at Reuters and Judith in the Rome branch of a Japanese fashion house. They were young and beautiful, enviable. Judith was much admired, not only by men but also by women; she was always at the center of attention. And yet every time she opened her mouth it was to say that she wasn't well. No one understood exactly what she had. She was affected by a mysterious ailment, or else she suffered from a kind of genetic wound, a birth scar, an original trauma. She was ontologically ill. She was a royal pain in the ass. But she did not try to kill herself. She used the threat of suicide as a weapon to elicit compassion. A dangerous weapon, more dangerous than Russian roulette. She shot herself in the temple, in fact, leaving Alfred a note that read:

"Now you will never be free of me. My death will haunt you for eternity".

Fifteen days later, Alfred too shot himself in the temple, with the same weapon.

Sandro Spigai gave a cocktail party for the opening of one of his shows. Actually it was given by one of his friends, Beatrice Finzi, one of his most loyal and solicitous consolers; he wanted nothing to do with it. He circulates among the guests with disgust.

For the occasion he inaugurated a new studio.

An imposing atelier: large whitewashed galleries, enormous glass doors (the towers of Villa Medici could be glimpsed from one of them), lofts, bookcases, archives, cabinets fit for a fashionable shop, large screen television sets, recorders, video recorders, virtual videogames, stereo, answering machines, fax, computer. Interior stairs lead to the terraces from which the rooftops of Via del Babuino command the view. To the right on the ground floor are a gym and rooms for Turkish baths and saunas, to the left enormous kitchens with electric ranges (Beatrice Finzi had also had him install these appliances, which she deemed suitable for a successful American painter; Beatrice does what she wants with Sandro, partly because she is his most patient listener when he tells the story about why he didn't die).

The studio is like a harem: models, photographic models, fashion models, assistants, secretaries, art school students, call girls, *natural born killers*, starlets, extravagantly tattooed sixteen year-olds with newborns on their shoulder, and twelve year-olds with pierced noses and tongues who circulate from one gallery to another like trampoline artists, or recline on the sofas displaying their semi-nude bodies and non-stop legs with an insolent, provocative look.

A young woman extricates herself from the crowd, and approaches the raised platform on which Sandro Spigai has his easels:

"I am the beautiful Sappho with hair the color of hyacinth" she says, imposing silence around her.

She has some sheets of paper in her hand, but she doesn't read, she recites from memory:

...seeing nothing,
Hearing only my own ears
Drumming, I drip with sweat;
Trembling shakes my body
And I turn paler than
Dry grass. At such times
Death isn't far from me.[3]

She runs her fingers through her hair, then she says:
"Now I am myself, Marta Cohen".
She recites, still from memory:

I am a daughter
Of chance (or chaos),
Of a failure of love,
Of a vacuum,
Of turbulent times,
Widowed of meaning.
Non-existent,

A-theist,
Pure Dasein,
Defection,
Vortex,
Undertow.
I am prey to violent passions,
The lust of predatory animals,
Of asps and hydras.
But I am a royal flower,
Fuchsia Splendens,
Digitalis Purpurea.
I hear the echo of distant voices,
Of tulips opening in the night,
The breath of birds in the nest.
I am a bird myself:
The bird of paradise,
Flapping my wings over the inferno.[4]

The guests who are closest applaud her; then they take copies of her verses from a table, and I do the same.

"This is one of my dearest friends" Sandro Spigai says to me as he introduces Marta Cohen. "I can't say if she is more beautiful or more intelligent".

Marta Cohen shakes my hand with a radiant smile.

"We already know each other: we often run into each other in Piazza di Spagna" I tell her.

"I work in Piazza di Spagna".

"I live there".

" I live in Via dei Greci, in a building without an elevator, on the seventh floor. Over a hundred steps, very high ones, the stairs of olden times. The building dates from the seventeenth century. It seems a cardinal lived there. I don't know how he did it with all those stairs. But for me they're worth climbing. I feel safer up there, in that tiny refuge in the sky".

18

"I live in a small attic, a hole in the wall, on the corner of Via Borgognona, but the building was recently renovated and has all the comforts: a modern elevator, a smartly dressed doorkeeper, closed-circuit television camera in the entry hall. Besides all that, I can see the church of Trinità dei Monti, the roof of the Hassler, and the house-atelier in which Giorgio de Chirico lived and worked, from the window which looks out onto Piazza di Spagna. According to what I read in a book, the painter would come down to the piazza like an aeronaut among wild savages".

"Cocteau wrote it... In any case, you're more fortunate than I".

"What work do you do, if I may ask?"

"She's a brilliant art critic" Sandro Spigai intervenes.

"What do you do?" Marta asks me in turn.

"I'm editor-in-chief of a new cultural magazine, "Ulysses 3000". In addition, I write literary and art reviews for the Rome daily "The New Tribune". The office of the magazine is on Via del Babuino, on the fourth floor, but there's an elevator there too".

"Did you study in Rome?"

"I graduated in Modern Literature at the University of Rome La Sapienza, with a thesis on language: on the relationship between the language of literature and that of painting, with particular reference to James Joyce for the first and Picasso for the second. But I wrote the thesis in a hurry, to finish as soon as possible... Then I spent two years in New York, where I did some occasional work for Italian television... It was in New York that I met Sandro Spigai..."

"How come you didn't applaud me?" Marta asks me unexpectedly.

"There was a big crowd around you" I reply, clearly embarrassed. I would never have imagined that she could have noticed that I had not applauded her.

"Didn't you like my poem?"

"Yes, of course…"

"Be honest".

"I was struck more by the way you delivered it than by the poem itself. You're a fascinating actress, you have a divine mouth" I tell her, inviting her to have something to drink and sit together in the corner.

She is wearing a black dress with black stockings and black high-heel shoes. Sitting down, her legs, sinewy with slender ankles, seem even longer. Her hands too are long and slender. Her mouth is sensual yet chaste, painted violet like her nails. Beneath the carmine red of her hair, her eyes dance with a restless light which is disturbing at times.

"I don't know if I should be flattered or offended by what you said".

"It doesn't seem offensive for a poetess to have a divine mouth. Maybe even Sappho had a divine mouth, besides hair the color of hyacinth".

"Of course, Sappho wrote divine poetry, while I… I would have liked to have learned Greek well enough to be able to read it in the original, but I was never able to…"

"How long have you been writing poetry?"

"I began writing when I was in high school, in Paris. The philosophy teacher was a young neo-existentialist who talked incessantly about Heidegger, Sartre, Camus. He demanded that we read *On Time and Being* at fifteen or sixteen years of age. While he explained it to us, I would write poems, to distract myself and avoid boredom. The poem that I read goes back to those years. It was an especially difficult period for me, because between fifteen and sixteen I suffered from anorexia, I was like a skeleton. Now I hate Heidegger. I just finished reading Elzbieta Ettinger's book about his relationship with Hannah Arendt. I was shocked by it. He behaved reprehensibly with Arendt. He used her to redeem his nazi past…"

"How come you studied in Paris?"

"I was born in Paris. My parents met in Paris. My father comes from an old Roman Jewish family, my mother is of Russian descent. My great-grandparents were Russian Jews, who landed in the French capital from Saint Petersburg on the day after the October revolution. My grandparents and my mother were also born in Paris. My father was a news correspondent for Italian television and my mother a fashion model. Then my father was called back to the home office and we came to Rome. I was eighteen years old, I had just finished high school. I enrolled in the Philosophy department, but then I got my degree in the History of Modern Art. I also took a course in Ancient Philosophy given at the Academy of France by a professor from the Sorbonne".

"What did you write your thesis on?"

"On Giorgio de Chirico, the de Chirico of the early Parisian period, the de Chirico of the *Enigma of Time,* of the *Red Tower,* of the *Song of Love*... De Chirico is my *amour fou*. I'm fascinated by his metaphysical skies..."

"He painted metaphysical skies but he frequented brothels".

"A lot of great artists loved brothels. Giacometti lamented their disappearance. In *The Atelier of Alberto Giacometti*, Jean Genet recalled that the sculptor would visit the brothels in adoration, and would actually get down on his knees before those whores, who seemed to him to be implacable, distant divinities".

"The first wife of de Chirico, Raissa Gourevich, would tell that her husband lost his head in Paris over a whore who frequented the Café de la Paix, near the Opera, and that their marriage fell apart because of it".

"De Chirico loved women of sumptuous corpulence, like the women in Renaissance painting".

"But the whore he lost his head over in Paris wasn't exactly like the women in Renaissance painting".

"These are the contradictions of an artistic genius. De Chirico hated the style of painting that he himself had helped create. Tanguy, Dalì, Max Ernst, Delvaux, Magritte derive from him. Mirò too was influenced by him. Even Balthus, the super-snob Balthus, owes something to him…"

"What does Balthus owe him?"

"He owes him what Walter Benjamin called 'aura'. Besides that, he's an ambiguous painter, extremely ambiguous. His nude or semi-nude children are detestable".

"I find them divine".

"They are obtuse little monsters, created by a perverse imagination".

"You're infatuated with de Chirico".

"Yes, I adore him. I have a lithograph of *Sun in a Fireplace with Self-portrait,* a girlfriend gave it to me when I graduated. I hung it on the wall in front of my bed, so that I can see it in the morning when I open my eyes. I never tire of looking at it".

"What do you do, other than look at *Sun in a Fireplace with Self-portrait* every morning? Sandro Spigai said you were a brilliant art critic. What newspaper do you write for?"

"I review art exhibits for the Milanese magazine 'Third Millennium', but it's bimonthly and I don't contribute to all of the issues. I spend most of the day in an art gallery in Piazza di Spagna. We sell paintings over the Internet…"

"An interesting job".

"An awful job. I'm sick of it by now… Besides that, I'm bored. In the evening, if I stay at home, I always reread the same books: fragments of Sappho, Baudelaire's *Les Fleurs du mal*, Rimbaud's *Une Saison en Enfer*… I also reread one of the novels of Georges Bataille, which I had read in French when I was seventeen or eighteen…"

"Which novels of Bataille do you like most?"

"None of them. Now I hate them. I only reread *My Mother*. I had promised myself not to read it anymore, but I always fall for it. It's stronger than I am… But I have less and less desire to read or reread. When I open a new book, I am seized by doubt: is it or isn't it worth spending the time to read it? In fact, I don't read it, I close the book... From time to time I also reread the poems of Sylvia Plath, especially the verses of *Lady Lazarus*.

Dying
Is an art, like everything else.
I do it exceptionally well.[5]

But I don't know that art well enough yet, I still have many things to learn from her" she adds, getting up with a sudden start.

"I have to go... If you want, we can see each other tomorrow evening".

"What time, where?"

"At 9:30, at Caffè Greco".

THE TEMPLE OF THE SUN

I'm at Caffè Greco, on Via dei Condotti.

The place is overcrowded, but you can still feel the spirit of the great ones who have passed through in the course of time: Goethe, Schopenhauer, Gogol...

I came twenty minutes early to get the table at which Giorgio de Chirico used to sit. I wanted to surprise Marta. When I arrived it was taken, but then it became free and I grabbed it. It's one of the tables in the first room, on the right as you enter.

I ordered a Punt e Mes.

Marta arrives on time.

She's wearing a green dress with white high-heel shoes, a strand of white pearls with a small emerald around her neck.

"You look fabulous".

"I dressed elegantly for you".

"You're naturally elegant".

" You're too kind".

"Let's see if you know: who always used to sit at this table?" I ask her as soon as she sits down.

"Who?"

" Giorgio de Chirico".

Marta gives me a kiss.

"I knew he came here often, but I didn't know that he had a specific table".

"He came here every day, around eleven. This was his table. The waiters wouldn't let anyone else sit here. One of the waiters who served him is still here. He told me that he always had the same aperitif: a Punt e Mes".

Marta notes that I am drinking a Punt e Mes and smiles at me. "A Punt e Mes for me too" she tells the waiter.

The Punt e Mes is brought by the waiter who used to serve Giorgio de Chirico; I ask him to tell us about the painter.

"He seemed like a Spanish nobleman" he recalls. "He didn't like being recognized, he didn't want to be bothered. He would watch everyone furtively with his slanted eyes. He always had a frowning, threatening expression, but he was really a happy soul, a great joker. He would stay here until around one, then go back home. Sometimes his wife came to pick him up and they would go to lunch at La Capricciosa, the restaurant at Largo dei Lombardi, on the other side of Via del Corso".

We thank him, and he goes away.

"He's right" Marta remarks. "He had an extraordinary sense of humor. He was completely misunderstood. They tore him apart: the de Chirico of the early Parisian period was genial, the de Chirico of the successive periods was awful. It was a vulgar operation, worthy of butchers. André Breton and Paul Eluard were responsible, since they had made an economic investment in the paintings of the early Parisian period and it was in their interest to devalue those of the successive periods. But metaphysical elements can be found in all of his work, even in paintings of the Sixties and Seventies. A painting like *Temple of the Sun* drives me wild. I would like to live in a place like that. Picasso used to say that Matisse had a sun in his belly, de Chirico had a sun in his head".

I notice that Marta has a small pin in the form of a sun on her dress.

I ask her if she wants another drink.
"Another Punt e Mes" she says.
I order two more Punt e Mes.

25

"You have an awesome memory".

"I've read the *Memoirs* of de Chirico three or four times, just as I've read *Hebdomeros* three or four times, the novel he wrote in the Twenties. He was also an original writer and a refined poet. You should read his books too, if you haven't already read them".

"Sorry, but I'm reading an extraordinary book right now".

"What is it?"

"Artaud's *Héliogabale ou l'Anarchiste couronné*. Artaud says that in Héliogabale's time the Tiber was a river of sperm, but now it's become a river of death".

"My parents live on the Tiber".

"I hope I didn't say something wrong".

"No, no... They live in the apartment where I lived too until three years ago. It's in the same building where Alberto Moravia lived, on the Lungotevere delle Vittorie. I would meet him often in fact, Moravia that is, when I went in or out. He was very nice, but arrogant. Each time he would ask me if I had read his books, which ones I had read, if I had liked them. It was an obsession, for him and for me. At first I didn't want to tell him that I hadn't read any of them, and I answered him vaguely, but he understood. He would invite me to his place saying: 'Come and see me, I'll give you my books'. I went two or three times, and each time I left with my hands full. He gave me *La mascherata, Il disprezzo, Io e lui, La vita interiore...*"

"And did you read them?"

"I read what was written on the flyleaf of the book jacket and then closed them up again. Before then I had only glanced at *Gli indifferenti*, when I was in my first year at University and hadn't yet met him in person... He was a funny man, he courted me ridiculously, he tried to establish contact with me by extending his arms and legs like an electronic manikin. I would burst into laughter and he would ask: 'Why are you laughing?' He had a morbid curiosity. I had the impression of being in a police station, or in a courtroom. He wanted to know everything about my life. He was looking for literary inspiration in me. He had lost his inspiration and he deluded himself that he could find it in the women he invited to come to his house or go out to dinner. I would often see different women entering his house, mainly foreigners... He was very bored, but he bored others much more than he bored himself. He would yawn continually, with no regard for his guests or onlookers. He would ask me: 'Have you read Elsa Morante's books?' or 'Have you read Dacia Maraini's books?' or 'Have you read Carmen Llera's books, and what do you think of them?' I would have liked to have said to him: 'Do you think I can waste my time reading these books?' In fact, one time I did tell him..."

"What did he say?"

"He exploded into fits of laughter."

Marta wants another Punt e Mes.

I order another two.

She fidgets because she can't smoke, and can't stop fiddling with the pack of Marlboros that she placed on the table as soon as she sat down.

"Why don't we go to La Capricciosa for supper?" she asks, after having finished the third Punt e Mes. She doesn't know that I already phoned the restaurant to reserve the table where Giorgio de Chirico used to dine.

We leave Caffè Greco as the purplish shadows of night are descending on Rome.

Even before reaching the door, Marta lights a cigarette and inhales a lungful as we walk along Via dei Condotti, glancing distractedly at the shop windows from time to time.

We reach Largo dei Lombardi.

The waiter who had spoken to me on the phone escorts us to the famous table.

It's one of the tables in the third room, in back, on the left, near the window with the etched panes.

The waiter recommends one of the house specialties.

Meanwhile the dining room has filled up. For the most part they are foreign tourists. Four young Japanese women are sitting at the table to our left, and another four at the table in front of us. All eight of them appear to be teenagers or very young, but it is difficult to say if they are fifteen or thirty. They eat with exquisite grace, and they speak in low voices as though they were in church.

"Have you ever been to Japan?" Marta asks.

"Once, two years ago, but I only visited Tokyo and Kyoto".

"They say that Tokyo is the New York of the Far East".

" Tokyo is a symbol of the current planetary delirium".

"I'm sure I would like it. I've wanted to go to Japan since I read a very beautiful novel, *The Setting Sun*. I bought it because I was attracted by the title, which reminded me of the setting suns of de Chirico, his metaphysical interiors, his Italian piazzas, his mysterious scenes. The author's name is Osamu Dazai. He killed himself".

"We could go to Japan together".

Marta doesn't answer.

"Wouldn't you like to go to Japan with me?"

"I'd like to go to Greece, to Volos, where de Chirico was born. I wanted to go when I was writing my thesis, but then I didn't have time any more".

"Then we could go to Volos together".

Marta gives me a kiss, this time on the mouth.

"To our trip to Volos" I say, inviting her to toast.

As I fill our glasses I realize that the bottle is almost empty, and I order another.

Marta eats with gusto and drinks without respite, to the point of keeping me constantly on the alert, since she doesn't fail to make me notice by her glance that her glass is empty.

28

"Sorry" I say each time.

"We could go to Volos in July, when I take my vacation" she proposes.

"Then I'll take my vacation in July too".

"Fantastic!"

Marta orders a selection of French cheese, and continues drinking and smoking. She drinks and smokes, or smokes and drinks, filling her glass herself and lighting her cigarette from the one that's still lit.

"I'm completely drunk" she tells me.

"Me too" I tell her so she won't feel uncomfortable.

But she doesn't seem to be able to notice discomforts of any kind.

"I detest alcohol, but I like to get drunk" she adds.

She calls the waiter in a loud voice and orders a whisky.

She drinks the whisky all in one gulp, then lowering her head and staring at the empty glass she says:

"My parents are two fucked-up shit-heads. They have never loved me, they brought me into the world without love, by accident. My mother would have liked to abort me because she was worried about losing her figure; she was afraid that pregnancy would ruin her body. She said motherhood filled her with horror, that she would never want to carry a strange body in her stomach. In fact she always treated me like I was a stranger, an intruder. I feel like a plant without roots, a reed in the wind. My mother hated my father, but she married him to get him to help her with her career.

She bursts into tears...

"I hate her, I hate her, I hate her!" she repeats sobbing...

She wants to drink some more, but I take her by the arm and convince her gently to leave with me...

She staggers.

I put my arm around her waist and accompany her to Via dei Greci 75.

PURE VERTIGO

I can't get to sleep.

I am wrestling with contradictory thoughts.

On the one hand I think that there was nothing I could have done but leave Marta at the door of Via dei Greci 75 and go away; on the other hand I think that under no circumstances should I have left her like that, not after she had revealed something deeply intimate to me and had gotten so upset.

Equally contradictory states of mind accompany the thoughts: first I feel composed, then troubled, everything going round and round in my head, incessantly.

Marta has bewildered me.

From the first time I saw her she seemed to be endowed with an innate style, such that she could never degrade herself, never lose that regal touch that set her apart like a genetic stigma, her personal heraldic coat of arms. But I had been forced to admit that this wasn't so. She was drunk, yes, completely drunk, as she herself had said. But I would never have imagined that she could lose her self-control to that point, on the contrary, I was sure that, even in the wildest state of inebriation, she would retain the light that was special to her, like a diamond shining among the ruins.

She had seemed to be at the point of crossing over the limit – that Pillar of Hercules of the personality – beyond which a human being is no longer recognizable in his identity.

30

Around three in the morning I get the idea of reading Bataille's *My Mother.*

The book grabs my full attention, and I continue reading for a long time until I collapse from exhaustion.

It's noon when I awake. I get dressed, pick up *My Mother* and go to the editorial office.

I sit at my desk and reread the book more carefully. As I read it, I recall what Marta told me about herself the night before, and through a spontaneous process of association of ideas, I compare her situation with my own.

I don't know if my parents conceived me with or without love, but I know something else, no less important. I don't remember ever receiving a caress from them, neither from my father nor – it's hard to believe – from my mother. But I never ached because of it. On the contrary, I always considered their emotional distance toward me a stroke of good luck, in that it released me from any form of gratitude toward them, from that obscene chain of *do ut des* – accusations, counter- accusations, blackmail, guilty feelings, recriminations – that shamefully binds children to their parents. My memories do not go beyond that. They are blacked out on this side of that obscure, prehistoric time in which the miracle or misdeed occurs. I could not say whether being conceived with or without love is a real problem or a metaphysical one, remote and unfathomable. I've never had the slightest urge to pose the question to myself, perhaps because I grew up too fast; I found myself all grown up before I knew it. But I've always had the sensation, since I was little, of walking on a tightrope suspended in air, like an acrobat but without a net to protect me, continually exposed to the risk of falling into the void. A sensation of absolute precariousness. Yet I hate all protective nets, any form of preventive safety measures, every type of self-defensive mechanisms.

31

Precariousness produces its awesome effect only if it is absolute. Only someone who has experienced it can say how it feels. It is a kind of vertigo of the mind, or of the spirit. Perhaps only the idea of nothingness produces the same vertigo, but the vertigo produced by absolute precariousness is immune from any kind of anguish. It is pure vertigo, or rather freedom from every bond, delirious intoxication, total unpredictability. Everything that had happened in my life until now was unpredictable, due exclusively to chance (or chaos, which is the same thing except for a slight difference in spelling)[6]. I even went to New York by chance, and the two years I spent there accentuated, if possible, the sensation of absolute precariousness that had pervaded me since childhood.

I feel like a reed in the wind and it doesn't bother me; Marta feels like a reed in the wind and grieves over it.

Paradoxically, a similar existential experience creates anguish and obsession in her case, freedom and delirious intoxication in mine.

Holding Bataille's book in front of me and leafing through it here and there, I tell myself that reading this book should have released Marta from the question of whether or not her parents had conceived her with or without love, assuming that she had really read and reread it. The protagonist of the novel, Peter, is not only conceived without love, but is born as a result of rape and is molested by his mother.

As Peter tells it:

I was born out of my father's casual lovemaking with my mother, who was fourteen years old at the time. The family had to marry off the two wicked youngsters, and the little wicked child had grown up in the chaos of that home.

His mother says to him:

My child, child of my forest! Embrace me: you come from

32

the leaves of the forest, from that fresh dew that I enjoyed, but I didn't want your father, I was bad. When he found me naked, when he raped me, I scratched his face until it bled, I wanted to tear his eyes out. But I wasn't able to.

In addition his mother tells him in a letter:

As I write to you I am seized by this delirium: my entire being shrinks inside me, my anguish screams within me, it tears me from myself as I tore you from me by giving birth to you. In the spasm of my shame, only a cry of hatred remains, more so than love. Anguish and desire devour me. It's not love; there is only rage in me. It was rage that brought you into the world, that rage which is now silent, but whose cry you recognized yesterday, as I could see by looking at you. I don't love you, I remain alone, but you hear that desperate scream, you will never stop hearing it, it will never cease to tear you apart; and I will live like this until I die.

"I don't know Marta's mother, but she couldn't be any worse than Peter's mother" I say to myself. "On the other hand, neither Peter nor Marta are the only ones to have been conceived without love. Who can say he was conceived with love nowadays? You're born by chance, and you live in chaos, like Peter".

The fact is that Marta doesn't want to speak to me anymore.

I called her several times at the gallery, but an anonymous voice answered abruptly:

"Ms. Cohen isn't here. We don't know where she is, nor when she will return to work".

"I'll wait for her tonight outside the entrance to the gallery" I tell myself.

I put aside *My Mother* and get to work.

Although the subject I'm writing about – "Ezra Pound and Venice" – interests me very much, progress is rather slow.

The Town Council of the city on the lagoon has prepared an exhibition of the American poet's Venetian memoirs and possessions from his estate on the top floor of a building on the Grand Canal. From the windows of those galleries one can admire one of the more evocative views of Venice, between the facade of the church of Santa Maria del Giglio, the Hotel Gritti and the bell tower of the church of San Maurizio.

The building stands a short distance from the place where Ezra Pound lived. He was then a young poet with an uncertain future, who, after a dangerous trip across the Atlantic on board a ship meant only for livestock, with barely eighty dollars in his pocket, was tempted to throw into the sea the manuscript of *A lume spento*; these verses, which he printed afterwards at his own expense, were later to rescue him from the crisis and signal a turn in his destiny.

The poems were dedicated to the painter William Brooke Smith, but in reality were addressed to whoever loved beauty in the same sense that he himself loved it.

Later, in The Pisan Cantos, the poet asked himself what he had done to deserve to live in a city as marvelous as Venice, and what he would have to pay for this privilege.

O God, what great kindness
Have we done in times past
and forgotten it,
That thou givest this wonder unto us
O God of waters? O God of the night.
What great sorrow
Cometh unto us,
That thou thus repayest us
Before the time of its coming?[7]

34

But Venice is more than marvelous.

Every time you see it again, it's as though you were seeing it for the first time: it 's always identical to the way it was, yet always new, always surprising.

It is a source of light that refracts in radiations and transparencies between sea and sky.

It is enveloped in mysterious veils, like Titian's *Venus*.

It reveals itself in successive layers, like Salome, but infinitely so.

Every year it sinks a little more, but the more it sinks, the more it rises up in the sky, like a mirage, a Fata Morgana, a celestial Jerusalem.

"Even Marta has a bit of Salome about her" I tell myself.

Only toward six do I finish the article.

It's around seven thirty. I am outside the gallery where Marta works. I'm sure she's in there.

After a few minutes Marta comes out.

She pretends she hasn't seen me, but instinct betrays her: what gives her away is a sudden emotion, like a start. She stops for a moment, giving me the impression that she would like to go back inside. Instead she comes toward me smiling, as if we had made a date to meet.

"Thanks for coming to pick me up".

I invite her to have a drink at Caffè Greco.

"I would prefer someplace where I can smoke".

We go to a bar on Via della Croce.

I'm moved. It's as though I were seeing her for the first time, or at least that's how it feels. She has fully regained her self-control, that power of seduction that emanates from her figure, her glance, her smile. She has a luminous air. Maybe she didn't expect me to go looking for her, or meet her at the gallery; maybe she had convinced herself that it was all over between us.

"I'd like a Glen Grant" she says, lighting a cigarette.

I order two Glen Grants.

"Forgive me for last night, I was really depressed".

"You forgive me".

"What did you do after you left me?" she asks, putting the emphasis on the word "left".

"This morning I had to write an article on the exhibit 'Ezra Pound and Venice'. I did some research, then I went to bed".

"I couldn't sleep. It was after three when I finally got to sleep. Now I'm a little tired. If you'd like, we could eat something at my place, but I have nothing in the house".

"We'll buy something" I tell her.

"First I'd like another whisky though".

I order two more Glen Grants.

"I don't want to talk to you about my parents any more" she tells me while we drink our second whisky.

"I don't see why you shouldn't talk to me about them".

"The problems are too personal, too intimate".

"Whatever you say".

"You want to wash your hands of it?"

"No, not at all, but it doesn't concern me much".

"Since I already spoke to you about it, it concerns you too now ".

"I've never had any relationship with my parents, except for a strange, brief experience with my father when I was ten years old, so it's hard for me to understand your problems".

"I too hope to break off relations with mine, but I don't know if I'll ever be able to do it".

"You're twenty-seven years old".

"Yes, but on the one hand I still feel like a child, while on the other I feel as though I were thirty-seven, forty-seven, fifty-seven".

36

We buy some Hungarian salami, curried chicken, French cheese, two bottles of wine and a bottle of Glen Grant.

Marta leads me into the dining room, asking me to put everything down on the table and open one of the two bottles of wine.

"You have a nice house" I say, approaching the window that looks out onto Via dei Greci.

"Thank you".

"I love airy houses, with little furniture, but I'm forced to live in a kind of monk's cell".

"But it's a cell that stands beneath the rooftops of the buildings of Piazza di Spagna. You're privileged" she tells me, inviting with me a look to pour her some wine.

"To us", I say, handing her a glass and raising mine for a toast.

"To our encounter, or rather to our re-encounter" she says, with a subtle irony in her voice.

She sets the table, then says to me:

"Excuse me a moment, I'll be right back".

She returns to the dining room slipping on a dressing gown.

Underneath it she's nude: no bra, no panties.

"What kind of music do you want to listen to?"

"Whatever you'd like".

I still like Gainsbourg, do you know him?

"Yes, of course".

"When I was in Paris, I was crazy about him. He was an extraordinary singer, a fabulous personality. He was called 'The Mephisto of the Year 2000'. He was a Russian Jew, he had a kind of fever burning in his blood. He died devoured by that fever".

As we eat and drink, Marta gets up continually under one pretext or another, letting her dressing gown fall open...

We continue eating and drinking – drinking more than eating – moving from the wine to the whisky.

She gets up again:
"Come, I'll show you my bedroom" she says.
On the wall in front of the bed is the lithograph *Sun in a Fireplace with Self-portrait*; on one of the side walls, a litho of Böeklin's *Island of the Dead*; on the other side wall, Max Klinger's engraving *On Death*; on the bed, a gold and black brocade bedspread.
"This bedspread was my great-grandmother's".
"It's very lovely".
"Do you like my bedroom?"
"It's very cheerful".
"Please don't be ironic".
"It inspires a great joy of living".
"Stop it".
"It's like *The Temple of the Sun*".
"I like it just fine… The bed is delightful" she says, sitting down on it and letting her dressing gown fall open again…
I sit down next to her, but she leaps up suddenly:
"Let's go get another whisky".

We go back to the dining room and I fill our glasses.

"I don't give a damn about my parents" she says, drinking half of her whisky.
"Parents don't exist", I say.
"Death to parents!" she adds.
"Let's toast their demise!"
"Great idea!" she exclaims, raising her glass.
All of a sudden she slips out of her dressing gown, caressing her body and running her fingers through her hair.
I make a move toward her, but she steps back:
"I'm sorry, but I'm dead tired" she says, showing me to the door.
I go down the stairs slowly, as she bolts the door.

38

DIANA, THE TEENAGER WITH THE HEAD
OF *GRUS CINERINA*

Via dei Greci is deserted.

Piazza di Spagna is submerged in a thick, dark fog; you can barely make out the shadows of the last ghostly figures crossing the piazza or milling around the steps. The church of Trinità dei Monti is enveloped in black smog.

I cross the square quickly and continue along Via di Propaganda, in the direction of Le diable au corps, the galactic discotheque and meeting place of the very young, of guys and girls in a frenzy.

I'm looking for Diana.

I've known Diana for four or five months.

I met her at the Accademia di Moda e Costume, the fashion school in Piazza Farnese where she was studying to be a designer. She was sixteen years old, but had grown up precociously, unfolding like a tropical flower. She was beautiful, tall and then some, sure and proud of herself. She surpassed the other students as though moving on a superior plane, in an atmosphere all her own, at an unattainable distance.

The apex of the flower was a biological portent: the head of a crane, the *Grus cinerina*, on an androgynous body, a long, lean face, rendered even thinner by an aquiline nose and a diaphanous pallor, animated however by brilliant blue eyes.

Although grafted onto the body with perfect symmetry, the head had a life of its own; it seemed to detach itself to wander through the sky, in lunar abstraction.

Handing me an album, she asked me if I could publish some of her designs in "Ulysses 3000". They were quite lovely, and I published four or five of them, introducing her as a sure promise. In a few months she shot to fame.

Now she designs for the most avant-garde, most outrageous designers.

She works free-lance.

She hates permanent jobs, having to go to a studio every day. She does her designs at home, when she feels like it, or when the fancy strikes her. She has a secret relationship with inspiration, which comes to her only in certain moments.

She has a multiple personality, each in total contrast with the other.

During the day she sinks into a lethargic inertia; at night she is repossessed by a frenzied energy.

She's like one of those flowers which close up at the end of the day and burst out again during the night.

She remains in hibernation until late in the evening. When night falls, she designs. Toward one in the morning she goes to the discotheque where she stays until the first light of dawn.

When I met her, she was living with her parents, but she didn't bother much about them. She was like a guest of the family; she considered her father's house a hotel, or a residence, while hoping to be able to get her own place to live soon.

The first time she came to my place, she called home at five in the morning to say that she would not be coming home. I don't remember who answered, whether it was her mother or the maid, but she simply said: "I'm staying out".

Another night she called home at seven in the morning.

Now Diana lives in the Frangipane Tower, the Torre dei Frangipane, in the center of Rome, in the vicinity of the Pantheon and near the church of Sant'Antonio, which con-

40

tains the works of famous artists, among them Canova. The Torre is also called "The Tower of the Monkey". According to legend, a baby girl newly born to the Frangipane family, the lords of the Palazzo, was saved and carried up to the tower by a monkey. The Frangipane, by way of thanks, installed a statue of the Madonna there, at whose feet a perpetual lamp has burned ever since.

The living space that has been created there is narrow, dark and asymmetrical: more like a crypt or catacomb up in the air than a dwelling. But Diana illuminates it during the day, and moves about with total ease and great agility, although there is nothing monkeyish about her except for the rapid start of her movements. She alternates the light, graceful step of a ballerina with the skipping hop of a magpie. She goes down to the *centro* as though she were dancing, and when she has to go a long distance she travels the streets astride a Honda.

I've been in the crypt five or six times, and each time Diana has had a surprise in store for me. She always has hashish or coke and offers it to her guests as a prelude to the night's events. The third time she brought Angela with her, one of her contemporaries from the Accademia who also diligently frequents the Diable au corps. After having overdone it with the drugs, they staged an erotic scene in my honor.

Angela dressed up like Lola-Lola from the *Blue Angel*: black stockings and garters, lace panties, sequined blouse, her eyes rimmed in black and her lips scarlet. She sang while straddling a chair: "I'm made for love from my head to my toes".

Diana undressed and assumed the pose of Ida Rubinstein painted by Serov: seated upright on the carpet of the little living room, her right leg crossed over her left, the ankle of her right foot wrapped in a green shawl which trailed along the carpet like a tropical snake, and the toes of her right foot crowned by a multicolor ring on reddish toenails. Her left hand rested on the carpet and the right hand dangled over the shawl, each hand sparkling with rings of white, whitish-blue, and opaque stones, her fingernails polished white and red. Her black hair fell over her left shoulder, onto her forehead and over eyes rimmed in black in a pallid face barely touched by the carmine of her lips.

Though Angela's appearance fell short of her role model, Diana outclassed hers: her legs were even longer, her face more enigmatic, her body more sinuous, her hair more lofty and weightless, winged. In addition she had tattoos on her arms and on her abdomen which replicated Klimt's designs, as well as a tattoo with the initials of her name and another in the form of an eclipse of the moon.

The crypt was in half-shadow, barely lit by the moonlight that filtered in through the attic window.

"Marlene" and "Ida" looked at each other for a long time, in silence, in a disturbing tension.

Angela got up from her chair and laid Diana on the carpet, biting her entire body and groaning with pleasure.

Diana got up from the carpet and swapped the roles, encircling Angela with her long winged body, clasping her between her coils, shrieking with sensual pleasure.

Worn out and exhausted, Angela stretched out on the carpet and lay there inert, unmoving as though dead.

Diana flew over and glided onto my sex, unleashing herself with her divinely obscene mouth.

An extreme sensation, unbearable.

Diana and I see each other exclusively at Le diable au corps. She's there every night, I go from time to time, especially when I want to see her. We notice our reciprocal presence from a distance, as though we had radar.

It's the radar that guides us.

An unspoken understanding has been established

between us: when we meet, we abandon any potential partner. And when the discotheque closes, we go to my place or hers, usually alone, unless we decide on the spur of the moment to invite some friends, male or female, should we go to her house.

Le diable au corps is going full blast.

Hundreds of delirious youths – guys dressed in black, tattooed and striped, young women half-undressed, disheveled, semi-naked, or adorned like post-modern Nefertitis, Cleopatras, Bathshebas – unleashed by ecstasy and other drugs.

A flaming aerial entanglement: floodlights, revolving cameras, strobe lights, gigantic photos of male and female nudes amidst smoking halos, flashes of fire, waves of lunar light, bluish, greenish, milky, reflective panels that dizzily multiply the bodies in psychomotor excitement.

An incandescent atmosphere, suited to stellar disintegration, planetary catastrophe.

A gigantic collective orgasm, set to the rhythm of electronic rock.

Diana steps out of the bedlam and comes toward me.

"I had a feeling you would come" she says kissing me.

There's fire in her mouth.

"Let's get something" I say, inviting her to the stand where the bar is.

"I'd like a gin and tonic", she tells me.

I order two gins and tonic.

She drinks hers quickly, asking me to order her another.

"I was dying of thirst" she says.

She's wearing a black leather miniskirt, black shoes, no stockings, and a blue top; her abdomen is bare.

"Let's go" I say, as soon as she's finished her second gin and tonic.

"To the dance floor?"

"I'd rather leave".

"Whatever you say".

She collects her quilted jacket from the coat-check, and we leave.

Without asking her if she wants to go to the tower or my place, I set out toward Piazza di Spagna, walking ahead of her.

Piazza di Spagna is still submerged in fog, but a thin purplish line is breaking through the shadows above the church of Trinità dei Monti.

She quickens her pace and comes up beside me.

Her body is burning.

At the corner of Via Frattina, I notice a half-open doorway: I push her into it and force her to kneel at my feet...

She goes back out to the piazza stamping her feet, infuriated:

"I didn't think you were so thoughtless, so violent! You broke the spell".

She turns back, running at breakneck speed.

I go back home, agitated and upset.

I go right to bed, but sleep badly: I toss and turn nonstop, until I plunge into a troubled, fitful sleep.

When I wake up, around eight, I try to remember what I dreamed.

I seemed to be in a kind of *Garden of Delights*, surrounded by beautiful naked women who vied to bestow their charms upon me, but an unusual female figure, under the guise of Diana the huntress, the mythical goddess, was piercing me with poisoned arrows, making me scream in pain, while another female figure, who resembled Marta, was kneeling gently at my feet, making me delirious with pleasure.

But I can still hear the echo of the abrupt clicks with which Marta bolted her apartment door behind me.

NO ONE WILL EVER LOVE ME

I woke up at eight because Marta called me.

Her phone call surprised me; I wasn't expecting it, especially at such an odd hour.

"I want to see you, I have to talk to you" she says.

"If you're not busy tonight, I can come and pick you up at your house at nine and we can have supper together".

"Let's say eight thirty".

When I heard her voice on the phone, I thought she wanted to say something to me about the night before. But I was wrong. Nothing, not a word.

I would have liked to take advantage of her call to get up and go to the editorial office, but I just couldn't. I stayed in bed, awake, thinking about the frustrating night and the dream I had had.

Only toward ten thirty did I get up. I had coffee, then went to the editorial office where I remained until evening, except for a short break to have a snack.

"I'm ready, I'll be right down" Marta tells me as soon as she answers the intercom.

She kisses me very gently, but her smile has something deceptive about it.

I propose that we go to the Birreria Viennese on Via della Croce, telling her that there's a violinist there and we could relax, but she objects saying she has to talk to me, as she had said on the phone.

We go to the restaurant on Piazza Mignanelli, near the Accademia Valentino and the steps of Trinità dei Monti.

"I'd never been here, it's very pleasant" she says looking around, even before we are seated.

We sit in a quiet corner and order…

I'm curious to know what she wants to talk to me about, but I refrain from pressing her.

There is a long pause…

"Cat got your tongue, Marta?"

"Your article on Ezra Pound is awful!" she blurts out.

"What?"

"You speak of him as though he were a great poet, but he's mediocre and boring. I've never been able to read him. He makes me nauseous".

"But there are many people who think he is a great poet, Marta. Hemingway considered him a very great poet".

"Pound is great all right, very great, but as a plunderer. The *Pisan Cantos* are a grotesque caricature of the *Divine Comedy*. An illegible pastiche. He was a detestable person, with that air of a great Indian saint in love with his own ego and possessed by his own idiocy".

"Marta, you're confusing the poet with his ideas, with what he thought".

"*The Thinker* of Rodin! He was a nazi-fascist idiot, an unrepentant anti-Semite".

" Céline and other writers and poets were also anti-Semites, but they weren't bad writers or bad poets because of it".

"But neither Céline nor the other great anti-Semitic writers and poets had written nazi-fascist propaganda or compared a good-for-nothing like Mussolini to a Renaissance commander".

"Not even Dostoievsky liked the Jews".

"Did you just discover that?" she asks me with a sarcastic laugh.

I motion for the waiter to come over.

The waiter brings us the menu again.

Marta goes back to reading it.

She orders a "pastiche" of macaroni, saying:

"Just to stay on the subject".

"You're ridiculous" I want to say to her, but she adds:

"Even Venice becomes squalid when described by Pound. An oily city, full of pigs".

"Enough, Marta, please".

"It would have been better if he had really thrown the manuscript of *A lume spento* into the sea".

"You're right, Marta".

By the time we leave the restaurant Marta can hardly stand up.

At the door of Via dei Greci 75 she says, ironically, making as if to shake my hand:

"Thank you for the lovely evening, goodnight".

"Don't you want me to come up?"

"Such condescension!"

As soon as we get upstairs, she says:

"Excuse me a minute, I'll be right back".

She comes out of the bathroom naked, her body sprayed with a provocative perfume.

"Marta, put on your dressing gown and let's have a whisky".

"Come on, get undressed!"

"Why in such a hurry, Marta?"

She begins to undress me herself, throwing my jacket on the floor and almost tearing off my shirt.

"Calm down, Marta".

"Your reflexes are a little slow" she comments in a sardonic tone as she strips off my pants and the rest.

"Let's go!" she adds, grabbing me by the arm and leading me to her bedroom.

She pushes me onto the bed and bends over me, puncturing me with furious bites, from my head to my toes.

I can hardly get out from under her fury.

She's implacable.

Only when I surrender, desisting all reaction and lying inertly on the bed, is she appeased.

She slips on her dressing gown and goes back to the living room, lighting a cigarette. I follow her; I too get dressed, and relax on the sofa.

"Do you want a whisky?" she asks me.

"Yes, thanks".

She hands me the glass and sits in front of me, with a questioning look.

"I still haven't understood something" she says.

"Lucky you: there are many things I still haven't understood".

"Please don't be ironic".

"What is it you still haven't understood?"

"I don't understand what you want from me".

"I want to be serviced".

"Your irony is distasteful".

"I'm a masochist".

"You're a narcissist, non a masochist! You want to be seen in public with a beautiful, elegant Russian woman".

"Yes, but at what price".

"Nothing is too costly for your vanity".

"Even vanity has a limit".

"The truth is you don't like me".

"On what do you base that conclusion?"

"If you liked me, you wouldn't have abandoned me at the front door the other night".

"The following night you put me out the door".

"That was a reaction".

"Was tonight a reaction too?"

"Yes, tonight too: I had the feeling you had no desire to make love with me".

"I've been attracted to you from the first moment I saw you".

"But what is it that attracted you?"

"Attraction is a mysterious phenomenon".

"Then why don't you want to make love with me?"

"Maybe our timing is different. You said yourself that my reflexes are a little slow, at least with respect to yours".

She gets up, refills the glasses with whisky, and sits down next to me saying:

"Andrea, you still haven't understood something fundamental".

"What is this fundamental thing?"

"That I want to be loved. Up till now no one has ever loved me. They've all been worthless affairs. One idiot courted me because he hoped that my father would find him a job in television, but when he realized that my father didn't really give a damn about me, he stopped coming around. Another idiot played on my mother's jealousy, but I don't know what happened between them because I left home. Only a young man whom I met at the gallery had some real interest in me, maybe. He was a painter and a poet, but he suffered from nerves and disappeared; I don't know what happened to him".

Marta becomes sad. She almost has tears in her eyes.

"No one will ever love me" she whispers.

"Marta, you should have more faith in life" I tell her, caressing her hair, without the slightest conviction.

"I don't have faith in anything or anybody. Is it possible you still haven't understood that?"

"That I understood, Marta".

"I, on the other hand, still haven't understood what you want from me".

"Maybe you're tired, Marta. Go to bed, we'll see each other tomorrow" I say, giving her a kiss.

"Go ahead, go! Get rid of me, you too!" she shouts, getting up and pointing to the door.

Only when I get home do I realize what she has done to me. There are bloody scratches and black bruises all over my body. I can't extend my arm, stretch out my leg, or bend over. I can't even turn over. I'm forced to lie supine in bed, motionless, like someone who's been wounded in battle.

THE END OF THE WORLD IS NEAR

Today Marta called me three times. She was nervous; she wanted to talk to me. I told her I would pick her up at her house at eight thirty this evening, and that we would take our time talking. She asked if we could meet earlier, but I told her I had work commitments. She insisted, but I repeated that we would see each other for supper. She hung up abruptly.

"Where do you want to go?" I ask her at eight thirty at the front door to Via dei Greci.
"Wherever you want".
"Why don't we go to Via Veneto?"
" Via Veneto is a dead street".
"But it's full of people".
"Like the cemeteries on All Souls day".
"You're in a sparkling mood today".
"The whole city is a cemetery, invaded by Holy Year pilgrims. I read in the newspaper that Rome has become the supermarket of the soul, but Rome has no soul".
"You're right, Marta, but let's make up our minds. Where do you want to go?"
"You've already decided: let's go to Via Veneto".

Marta hates Rome. For one thing she hates it because her parents brought her there without asking her, leaving her to face a *fait accompli*. She would have liked to have remained in Paris, to have lived in Paris where she had friends from childhood and adolescence, even though she had suffered from anorexia there and had been reduced to a skeleton, as she herself had said. Certainly for a woman like her, who has a desperate need to see herself and others clearly – herself more than others – it's not easy to live in a city as ambiguous, deceptive and cynical as Rome. She sees it as a dead city, and she's not entirely wrong. It's an immense necropolis, with its underground loaded with tombs, catacombs, crypts, pagan and Christian basilicas, its subterranean life swarming with ghosts and specters, the wandering shades of saints and martyrs, spirits or *revenants*, who night and day erupt into real life, so that the dead cannot be distinguished from the living, nor the living from the dead, the saints from the criminals and the martyrs from the executioners. It's an infernal city, infested with demons, dragons, prostitutes clothed in gold as in the *Apocalypse* of Saint John. But it is also a divine city, a "city of the sun", with radiant light, sunsets of yellow gold or purple violet, skies filled with angels and Christs like those of El Greco, dominated by domes of gold or green copper which sketch a surreal or abstract architecture in space. But Marta sees only its mortuary dimension.

"Here's your Via Veneto!" she says sarcastically as we get out of the car at the corner of Via Ludovisi, in front of the Hotel Excelsior.

We stop at the Café de Paris, one of the places in which *la dolce vita* used to reign, taking a table outside.

A waiter hurries over to offer us menus, as we watch people passing by, in one direction and the other.

"Why didn't you want to see me earlier? What was it you had to do? Maybe you had to write an article on another great anti-Semitic poet?" Marta asks with a treacherous smile.

"Marta, you're becoming more of a bore than Ezra Pound".

"In that case, I'll go".

"Go then".

She gets up, then she thinks it over and sits down again.

"Marta, please, stop the business with Ezra Pound. What did you want to talk to me about?"

"I wanted to talk to you about my work. I can't take that gallery any more".

"We'll look for another job".

"What kind of job?"

"We'll find another newspaper for which you can write about art".

"What art? After Giorgio de Chirico's death, all you find in Rome and Italy are his inept imitators, his more or less distorted nephews".

"But you already write for 'Third Millennium'".

"Yes, but three or four articles a year and only what the editor wants".

The waiter is still waiting.

"What would you like to drink?" I ask her.

"Whatever you want".

"Is champagne all right?"

"To celebrate what?"

"Your future job".

"There is no future job for me, in fact there isn't even a future".

The waiter goes away.

Marta is right: Via Veneto is a dead street, I say to myself as I watch the passersby.

They walk as though they were in a funeral procession. The newsstands and terraces along the street seem like funerary monuments; the only things missing are the epigraphs with the photos and names of the deceased.

The waiter approaches again.

"What would you like, Marta?"

"I don't want anything".

The waiter goes away again, shaking his head.

"Marta, you could write for 'Ulysses 3000', with no restrictions".

"Andrea, I thought you were more sensitive than that. What I wanted from you was the advice of a friend, not an assignment for your magazine".

"I'm sorry".

As the waiter once again hands us the menus, a young man storms over to our table:

"I'm Jack Cooper, excuse me if I'm bothering you" he says, speaking with difficulty because he is panting; his Italian is correct but mangled by an American accent.

"No, please" Marta says, with curiosity.

"I'm sorry to tell you, but you two are insecure, disturbed, unhappy. I can read it in your eyes..."

Marta and I laugh...

"You're afflicted by a profound malaise, whose cause you yourselves are unaware of..."

We laugh again...

He appears to be around twenty-five, but maybe he's even younger. He has eyes which are a pure, clear blue, tawny blond brows and eyelashes, odd features, and a freckled face. He's wearing a blue suit, white shirt, a polka dot tie, and red shoes with the heels worn down on the outer side. Over his shoulder he carries a black leather pouch equipped with pockets, sub-pockets, little pockets, belts and buckles.

He lifts the pouch with his right hand and takes it off, letting it fall at our feet.

"Excuse the intrusion, I'd like to sit down a minute and explain to you why you are insecure, disturbed, unhappy..."

"Please, sit down" Marta tells him.

"Thank you, but I want you to be honest with me".

"We will be" I say.

Marta laughs ironically, as though to say: "You'll never be capable of being honest".

"You answer him, since you're so honest" I tell her.

"You don't understand each other because you suffer from a profound lack".

"A lack of what?"

"You lack something essential".

"What?"

"Faith".

"Faith in who or what?"

"Faith in God".

"But God is dead" I tell him.

"Spare yourself the obvious" Marta says.

"Exactly, He died for our salvation. You have to regain your faith in God if you want to be saved" Jack Cooper tells us.

"How do you regain your faith in God?" Marta asks him.

"Through prayer".

"But I have no desire to pray" Marta tells him.

"Me neither" I say.

"Don't disturb us" Marta says to me.

"You have no desire to pray because evil has taken root in your will, in the dark depths of your being. You must come to us if you want to regain your faith in God".

"To you where, to whom?" Marta asks him.

"To the church of Jesus Christ and the Latter Day Saints. You must do it soon, because the final days are approaching. You might be too late".

"Where is the church of Jesus Christ and the Latter Day Saints?" Marta asks him.

"Here" he replies, taking a brochure from his pouch and offering it to us.

Marta glances at the brochure and hands it over to me.

There's a lengthy text, with the church's address at the bottom.

"What hours is the church open?" Marta asks him.

"All hours, even at night. But you must come to us

before the world is reduced to ashes and stone upon stone is not left standing".

"It wouldn't be a bad thing if Rome were reduced to ashes and stone upon stone were not left standing" Marta says.

"Not only Rome but the entire world" Jack Cooper says.

"It would be a magnificent spectacle" Marta says.

"Even John Paul II said that the end of the world was in sight, although our church, which is the only true church, has nothing to do with the church represented by the Pope of Rome. The prophets of our church will tell you how to regain your faith in God".

"We'll come" Marta tells him.

Jack Cooper gets up, takes a bunch of pamphlets from his pouch and puts them on the chair on which he has been sitting. He asks for our names, addresses and telephone numbers, writes them in a notebook, and implores us:

"Don't delay, for the love of God".

He slings the heavy pouch back over his shoulder, extends his hand with a smile, and starts off, but as he is crossing the street a car speeding in the wrong direction slams into him, hurling him to the other side of the street, toward the entrance of the Hotel Excelsior.

"Too bad, I liked him" Marta remarks, calling the waiter and ordering a glass of champagne.

Via Veneto becomes crowded with police cars and curious onlookers, but Marta barely gives a fleeting glance at the scene and calls the waiter back:

"I'd like some oysters" she says.

Now Marta is eating and drinking enthusiastically; she smiles, laughs, observes the passersby attentively, and speaks in a loud voice.

"In Paris" she recalls "a high school classmate jumped from the third floor of a building, but the doctor was able to save him. When he was released from the hospital, he jumped from the fifth floor of the same building, but the same doctor was able to save him a second time. So then he got a gun, and first he shot the doctor, then himself".

"Amusing" I say.

She laughs resoundingly, emptying the glass of champagne.

"Would you like anything else?" the waiter asks us.

"Marinated salmon" Marta says.

"Assorted antipasto and another two glasses of champagne" I say in turn.

"Now I'll tell you another story" Marta begins, but suddenly a woman appears in front of the Café de Paris, shouting in the direction of a man of about forty, who is standing near the newsstand with a wary, thoughtful and bewildered air:

"Impotent, crazy loser!"

She's no more than twenty, rather pretty, with long blond hair and dark eyes; she's flaunting a brand new silver fox fur.

She approaches our table.

Turned toward us, but as though speaking to the entire clientele, she says:

"I've never had anything like this happen to me. It's crazy! I was in front of the Hotel Ambasciatori, and he gestured to me with his head. I went with him to my car, I had him get in. I told him how much money I wanted, and he didn't object. I started the car and took him to an out of the way street, in Villa Borghese. I started to open his pants, but he stopped my hands. "Wait a while, I want to talk to you first" he said. I waited. He began to ask me a lot of questions: how old I was, what my father did, what my mother did, if I had brothers and sisters and what they did, if I was married, if I had children, who my pimp was, where I lived and with whom, he went on and on... He had a strange tone, like a priest, a father confessor, but I quickly caught on..."

She asks us for a cigarette. Marta lights it for her, and she continues:

"I'm an educated woman. I've studied. I spent three years in the boarding school for the protection of the daughters of Mary on Via delle Vergini. I've read the life of Saint Maria Goretti, the life of Saint Teresa of the Baby Jesus, the life of that French saint, what's her name? I can never remember her name. Sister Angelina even made me read the *Confessions* of Saint Augustine, but after a while I stopped because I couldn't understand a thing. I realized right away that that faggot didn't want to make love, he wanted to redeem me, lead me back to the straight and narrow, that's exactly what he said, the straight and narrow. Imagine such a thing! Redeeming someone like me! I'm the queen of sex! I told him to shove off, to think about saving himself and leave me in peace. I would have liked to have left him there, among all those queers, but then I felt sorry for him and I brought him back to Via Veneto. But now he won't leave me alone: he tags after me, he watches me, he follows me like a cop. The moment I turn around, he reappears behind me, making it impossible to work..."

She apologizes for the intrusion and goes off, passing through the crowd with a triumphant arrogance.

"She's right" Marta remarks.

"Shall we go to your place or mine?" I ask Marta.
"I'd prefer mine".

She climbs the stairs without stopping to take a breath; she's happy, euphoric.

"Sit down" she tells me, indicating the couch in the living room.

"What do you have to drink?"

"I have no champagne, I'm sorry; I have an Italian spumante".

She fills two glasses, hands me one and sits at the table.

"Would you like some hashish?" she asks, lifting her glass.

"Why not?"

"I have some that's of especially high quality, a girlfriend brought it to me from London".

"Let's try it".

"But first a little music" she says, getting up and sliding a Gainsbourg cassette into the stereo.

She prepares two cigarettes and offers me one.

"I don't smoke it if it isn't pure" she says.

"I smoke what I can get".

"You shouldn't".

"I'm not so sophisticated".

"But you smoke sophisticated hashish".

"I smoke a little of everything".

"Hashish only has its effect if it's pure".

"What effect?"

"Calming the nerves, if not the soul".

She finishes her cigarette before me.

I finish mine too and ask her to roll another two, but she shakes her head with a nervous gesture.

"Please, Marta".

"Can't you see I'm getting bored?"

"Maybe it's the effect of the pure hashish".

"It's you who are boring me!"

"Marta!"

"You bore me to death!" she shouts, getting up suddenly, taking off her jacket and blouse, and leaving her breasts bare.

I get up in turn and go toward her, but she takes off her skirt, steps out of her shoes flinging them in the air, slips off her panties and throws them in my face:

"I'm not a strip-tease artist, I don't do strip-tease! Get out, go find a whore!" she screams, opening the door.

"DIANA'S MIRROR" AT NEMI

Marta calls me at seven.

"I'm sorry to wake you so early, Andrea, I wanted to apologize for the other night" she says, adding in a falsely contrite voice:

"I feel guilty, I behaved indecently. I don't know how to make you forgive me".

"Fuck you, Marta".

"Forgive me, Andrea, I beg you".

"Marta, go to hell".

"Don't hang up, please. One more minute, just one minute. I also wanted to ask you to go to Nemi with me. I have to go there to see if Palazzo Ruspoli would lend itself to putting up art shows there. I should have gone several days ago, but today I absolutely must go. The manager of the art gallery where I work won't stop bothering me. Why don't you come with me?"

"No, Marta".

"We can leave around ten. It will be a nice outing, you'll see".

"I don't feel like an outing, Marta".

"Have you ever been to Nemi?"

"No, Marta, I don't even know where it is".

"It's an enchanting village, a mysterious place. We could see the ruins of the Temple of Diana, the goddess of the hunt".

"I already see more than enough ruins in Rome, Marta".

"The lake of Nemi, which is called 'Diana's Mirror', is full of prehistoric ruins and human remains".

"The prehistoric ruins and human remains of the Tiber are enough for me, Marta".

"Do you know Frazer's *Golden Bough*?"

"No".

"Do you know Turner's *Golden Bough*?"

"Turner, who?"

"Don't act silly, Andrea, please. The 'golden bough' that grew in the sacred wood of Nemi was closely watched over by the *rex nemorensis*, who reigned until he was killed by someone stronger and craftier than he, and so on and so forth, one killing after another, in an endless chain".

"Just like in today's Rome, Marta".

"In order to kill the *rex nemorensis*, the emperor Caligula had enlisted an invincible mercenary".

"Who did he recruit, Schwarzenegger?"

"Virgil spoke about the 'golden bough' in the Aeniad. He said that Aeneas, following the advice of the Sibyl, had to obtain the 'golden bough' and bring it to Persephone if he wanted to return from the realm of the dead".

"You can go to Nemi with Aeneas, Marta".

"Please stop being ironic, Andrea. I'll wait for you at ten in Piazza di Spagna near Bernini's Fountain".

Piazza di Spagna is already full of people, but Marta stands out from a distance in the morning sunlight.

She is dressed like Diana the huntress: a beige chamois miniskirt with fringes that adorn her legs, shiny black laced boots, a black leather jacket over a beige top with a violet foulard.

Her mouth too is violet: a blackish violet, funereal, like the shadows under her eyes, and her nails.

"Maybe she thought she was going to Transylvania" I think.

"Thank you for coming" she says, kissing me.

"Shall we go in my car or yours?" I ask, returning the kiss.

"I prefer mine, it's more comfortable and faster than your old Thema".

We get her silver Alfa from the garage on the hill to San Sebastianello.

It's the first time I've ridden in it, with her at the wheel.

We take off.

She advances recklessly into the chaos of the *centro*, but with a great deal of assurance and surprising control of the car.

Every time she performs a feat, she turns toward me smiling, as though expecting applause.

"You're phenomenal" I tell her.

She attempts to pass à la Schumacher.

I note that even her panties are violet.

We turn onto Via Appia.

Now she's driving more slowly; she seems to want to relax.

"Frazer's *Golden Bough* is a legendary book, as you know. The original edition consists of twelve volumes, but I also have the condensed edition. It's in my purse".

"I prefer books of twelve pages, or better yet, twelve lines".

"Very funny".

Every so often women in black tights appear on the side of the road sitting on rocks or standing with widespread legs around small pyramids of smoking logs, even though it's already spring.

"There they are, the priestesses of the Temple of Diana, we don't have to go to Nemi" I tell her.

"If you don't stop it, I'll go by myself".

"No, I was wrong, they are the neo-vestals who keep the sacred fire of Virginity burning".

"I'll make you get out!"

"Before we enter Via dei Laghi, I notice the ruins of the Roman aqueducts to the right. They stand outlined in the morning mist like giant human skeletons, as far as the eye can see.

"It's strange that a people who were as crazy about cleanliness as the ancient Romans were would have left us a city as filthy as today's Rome" I think, as Marta depresses and releases the accelerator, the violet of her panties in full view.

We turn onto Via dei Laghi.

"On the right is the seventeenth century villa belonging to Carlo Ponti and Sophia Loren" Marta tells me. "It stands within an endless wood, populated with exotic animals. The drawing rooms were filled with Picasso, Moore, Bacon, but then the customs agents seized them".

"The customs agents are the only ones in Italy who still have an interest in art".

"The customs agents and the thieves. In the gallery where I work we've already had three thefts".

"That's Marino" Marta tells me, indicating with a glance a little village up above, on the left.

"You see, you've found a new job! You're a perfect tour guide".

"Don't act silly, Andrea. I just want to make it up to you for having wakened you so early and for having involved you in this trip".

"It's a lovely outing, no doubt about it".

"You're really unpleasant today".

"Now what's the matter?"

"At the entrance to Marino is Paradise, the hunting lodge where Vittoria Colonna received Michelangelo".

"Vittoria Colonna flirted with Michelangelo?"

"No, of course not, Michelangelo loved Davids, you should know that at least".

We go up to Nemi.

"The manager of the gallery where I work would also like me to go to Monte Cavo, at the top of Rocca di Papa,

64

where there's an old monastery that's been transformed into a hotel" Marta tells me. "She'd like us to set up shows there as well. But now I'd like you to see the little church which contains a crucifix sculpted in the seventeenth century by Fra Vincenzo da Bassano with wood from Mount Calvary".

"Why don't you suggest to the gallery manager where you work that you set up exhibits on Golgotha as well?"

"Stop it, Andrea, please. You're getting on my nerves".

She enters Nemi like a shot, amidst shop windows and balconies adorned with baskets of strawberries and flowers, and pedestrians who jump onto the sidewalks swearing.

We reach Piazza Umberto I, on which Palazzo Ruspoli stands.

She parks along the uphill street that borders the Palazzo and we walk down to the piazza.

Near the newsstand a young man who is waiting for her says:

"The superintendent of City Culture was unable to come, and makes his apologies. He's working. He delivers mail to Ariccia, his second job, if not his first. Here we make a living cultivating strawberries and flowers, which we sell in Rome and elsewhere, but not everyone succeeds in balancing the budget. The superintendent sent me. I have the keys".

"It wouldn't be a bad idea if the superintendent of City Culture of the Commune of Rome would also do some useful work, maybe delivering mail to Ostia" I tell him.

The young man laughs; Marta laughs too, but through clenched teeth.

"This door with a Renaissance arch is magnificent" Marta says as we approach Palazzo Ruspoli, which is topped by a tall cylindrical tower.

The young man opens the door saying:

"It's admired by all the art historians, especially the architects. It's one of our marvels".

"It's an absolute marvel" Marta says.

We enter the Palazzo.

"Even the interior is magnificent, it would only have to be restored a bit, converted and illuminated" Marta says, walking back and forth, looking at the walls and ceilings.

"It's a magnificent nightmare" I say.

"Andrea, you're intolerable".

We go back to the piazza.

The young man says to us:

"If you want to have a nice lunch, I recommend the Specchio di Diana, an inn that's just a stone's throw away. It has two terraces from which you can enjoy an enchanting view of the lake, as far as Genzano and beyond, toward the sea. I'll walk you there".

The young man introduces us to the owner of the Specchio di Diana and says goodbye, telling us that he is at our disposition.

The innkeeper leads us to the first floor, giving us a table on one of the two terraces and telling us:

"This restaurant goes back to the second half of the nineteenth century. Famous people have eaten here. D'Annunzio had lunch here, right here on this very terrace. He was with Barbara Leoni. The poet's biographers have even recorded what they ate: bread, salami, wine, macaroni, cutlets with a side dish, fried fish, fennel, and coffee".

Marta says to him:

"I want to eat roast kid and wine made from black grapes and cakes served piping hot on grape leaves".

"The roast kid and dark wine we have, but I don't know

66

how to make cakes served piping hot on grape leaves. I've only been running this place for a short time".

"I read it in Frazer's *Golden Bough,* in the first few pages of the book" Marta replies. "I have the book here with me. If you'll be patient with me, I'll read you the passage in which Frazer talks about the cakes served piping hot on grape leaves".

"Of course, go ahead".

Marta takes the book from her purse, opens it and reads:

"At the annual festival of the goddess, hunting dogs were crowned and wild beasts were not molested; young people went through a purificatory ceremony in her honor; wine was brought forth, and the feast consisted of a kid, cakes served piping hot on plates of leaves, and apples still hanging in clusters on the boughs".[8]

She raises her eyes from the book and adds:

Frazer talks about the wine made from black grapes on another page".

"For now I'll bring you the wine" the innkeeper tells us, "I'll do my best about the piping hot cakes".

"The view of the lake is remarkable from here" Marta says.

The view of that lake fills me with anguished sadness, but I reply "it's more than remarkable".

"Here we are" the innkeeper says, setting down a carafe of dark wine and filling our glasses.

"It's divine" Marta tells him, putting her half empty glass back on the table...

The innkeeper refills her glass and says with visible pride:

"Byron also wrote about Nemi".

"I know, I know" Marta says, "I can remember some of Byron's poems from memory".

She empties the second glass and recites:

67

Lo, Nemi! navell'd in the woody hills / So far, that the uprooting wind which tears / The oak from his foundation, and which spills / The ocean, o'er its boundary, and bears / Its form against the skies, reluctant spares / The oval mirror of thy glassy lake; / And calm as cherish'd hate, its surface wears / A deep cold settled aspect nought can shake, / All coil'd into itself and round, as sleeps the snake.[9]

The innkeeper looks at her admiringly. He's almost about to applaud.

Marta smiles, pleased with herself.

"Byron, D'Annunzio, cutlets with a side dish, fennel, the glassy lake, the stuff of suicide" I say to myself.

"D'Annunzio writes about his amorous nights in the Castelli Romani with Barbara Leoni in *The Triumph of Death*" Marta says, continuing to guzzle the wine, one glass after another.

The innkeeper personally serves us the roast kid and brings us a second carafe of dark wine, telling us:

"The chef is preparing the piping hot cakes for you. He'll serve them to you himself on grape leaves".

"You are priceless" Marta tells him.

"You should thank the chef rather than me" the innkeeper replies.

Before the chef brings us the piping hot cakes on grape leaves, the second carafe is also empty.

"A little more wine, please" Marta says to the chef, after he has brought us the piping hot cakes on grape leaves and after she has started eating them.

"How are they?" the chef asks her, setting down a third carafe of wine.

"Thank you, thank you, they're delicious" Marta answers, continuing to eat and drink.

68

"You're not eating any?" the innkeeper asks me.
I try them too, they burn my mouth.
When we leave the inn, Marta is staggering.

"Now we'll go see the ruins of the Temple of Diana"
Marta says, indicating the arch where the road leading to the
right shore of the lake goes off; it is skirted along the first
stretch by a parapet on the left that serves as a panoramic
viewpoint.

We pass the arch and begin to descend.

"It looks like an immense Van Gogh" Marta exclaims,
leaning over the parapet and inviting me to look at the
expanse of narcissus in bloom, which from up above
stretches as far as the lake, passing through vineyards and
fruit orchards and nurseries set geometrically among the
trees.   ·
"It's true" I say, while in actuality that expanse of narcissus in bloom depresses me no less than "Diana's Mirror".
"Afterwards we'll also go see the ruins of the Roman ships
that Caligula had built" she says, walking along in the middle of the road, which is now devoid of a parapet and
opens, on the left, onto an abysmal void.
She skips along, straying from left to right, and right to
left, threatening to fall off the edge or end up being hit by a
car.
Every once in a while she stops suddenly, picks some
flowers – daisies, primula, anemone – and puts them in her
hair.

We reach the Garden where the ruins of the Sanctuary of
Diana stand.
There's nothing but stones blackened by time and bad
weather, desolate and desolating, set among wild plants and
prickly brambles.

But Marta is delirious.

"I feel like Diana the huntress" she shouts, caressing those black stones with her vampire fingers.

I would like to taste the mouth of a goddess, but I have the feeling that I would plunge into deadly anguish.

"Diana's Mirror" seems ever more odious to me.

"It's a burning glass" I say to myself.

"Marta, now we have to make the long climb back up".

"We still have to see the ruins of the Roman ships".

"We'll see them another time, Marta".

"You're always difficult".

I gesture with my hand at the first car that approaches us.

There's a woman at the wheel.

I ask her to give us a lift back up.

She lets us get in and drops us off at Piazza Umberto I.

Marta retrieves her car and we set off along the same downhill road.

"How happy I am, Andrea!" she says, looking at the panorama.

"Me too, Marta!"

All of a sudden she turns to the left and bursts through the expanse of narcissus in bloom, pressing the accelerator to the floor, climbing over the little walls surrounding the gardens, crushing the plants, trashing one nursery after another. She is headed straight for the lake but when she is about to reach it the car comes to a violent, jolting stop against two rocky spurs.

We too are jolted, banging our heads against the roof of the car.

The rear-view mirror shatters; the fragments splatter us with blood.

A farmer helps us get out and extricate the car.

70

We too are ruins, two relics of the Temple of Diana, or two heroes of the bloody legends that make this sacred place fatal I think, as the first evening shadows descend upon the lake.

"I'm sorry, I was blinded by the sun" Marta says. "All of a sudden I couldn't see anything and I lost control of the car".
But I am certain that she had decided to sink into "Diana's Mirror" with me.
A fatal, glorious death.

The car is covered with earth and leaves; the windscreen has been shattered, but the motor is intact.
We get back in.

She starts out smoothly, looking around, as though wanting to admire the panorama in the dusky twilight. But all of a sudden she accelerates, paying no attention to the curves and to the cars coming in the opposite direction. She slows down and speeds up again, uncontrollably, in an alternating rhythm, until having taken the road toward Rome, she performs in a crazy *gymkhana*.
Half-undressed, covered with blood, her lipstick smudged, her mascara running down her face, she seems to enjoy challenging the impossible, but all at once she stops the car on the side of the road and throws herself headlong against me…

She jerks violently.

We make the trip back to Rome in record time.

FAMILY, I HATE YOU

Marta wakes me at seven again.

"I couldn't sleep so I started to write. I wrote a poem. I want to read it to you".

"You can read it to me later, Marta. I'll call you".

"Why don't we see each other for lunch?"

"I'll come and pick you up at the gallery at one thirty".

"I can get away even earlier. Come at one".

We go to the restaurant on Piazza Mignanelli; we sit at the same table as last time.

Marta takes a notebook out of her purse.

"First let's order something" I tell her.

"I have no appetite today" she replies, handing me the notebook.

"Let's at least order something to drink; afterwards you'll feel hungry".

"Whatever you say".

I order two aperitifs.

"You read it" Marta says.

"I'd rather you read it. You'll read it better".

She opens the notebook:

"Family, I hate you" André Gide used to say.
But his hatred was balm compared to mine.
There are no words to say what I feel.
It's an inexpressible feeling, pure, infernal horror.
But my inferno doesn't last for only a season,
It lasts for an enormous, endless time.

Mine is a sentence as long as life imprisonment.
But with life imprisonment there is the hope of pardon,
I have no hope, there will be no pardon for me.
The prisoner has the illusion of escape,
The criminal has the honor of an identikit,
I don't know who I am, nor where to go.
"He who does not know where to go, goes further than
anyone else" says an old proverb. But I am already far
away: far away from myself, far away from others, far
away
From God. Even God has abandoned me.
I'm a falling star, lost in a dark sky.
I am a survivor in a stormy sea.

Animals have the warmth of their den,
Even the most ferocious animals bestow tenderness
Upon their young. I don't know warmth, I don't know
Tenderness. No gentle hand has ever touched
My tender skin, no loving breath
Has made my heart jump.

She shuts the notebook and raises her head, looking into my eyes.

"It's very lovely, it's like a ballad" I say.

"Do you really like it?"

"Very much".

She gives me a kiss.

"Have you reread Rimbaud?"

"I know Rimbaud by heart".

"Good for you".

"Let's toast then!"

I order two glasses of champagne.

"To your poem" I say, raising my glass.

"I'm happy" she replies, making her glass clink against mine.

"You were right: my appetite is back".

I call the waiter back.

"A T-bone steak" Marta tells him.

"But they're big, T-bone steaks are for two" the waiter informs her.

"Even better, we'll share it" Marta says.

The restaurant has filled up.

"I feel everybody's eyes on me, both the men's and the women's" Marta says to me.

"Your beauty is dazzling today".

"But what is beauty? 'I don't know what beauty is' Dürer used to say".

"Marta, perhaps you don't know what beauty is because you carry it with you and within you without being conscious of it, like a plant, or an animal".

"I'm not that blind".

"You're like *The Most Beautiful Lady*".

"You shouldn't quote Blok, but rather Esenin:

Dying isn't new under the sun,
But neither is living any newer.

"Marta, I must tell you that I could never stand Esenin: he was a ridiculous dandy, a citified farmer who hid the smell of the earth under French or American perfumes…"

"His only defect is that he was an anti-Semite".

"His suicide was inevitable, as was Duncan's for that matter".

"But Duncan didn't kill herself".

"Hers was an unconscious suicide".

"In any case, I have nothing to do with *The Most Beautiful Lady*. What good is beauty to me? Up till now it's only brought me suffering. Everybody wants me, nobody wants me".

"I don't understand, Marta".

"Men are immediately attracted to me, but then they all disappear, all of them, and I find myself alone again, more alone than before".

"I won't disappear, Marta".

"You'll disappear too".

In the time I've known her, I've never felt as attracted to Marta as I do today. Marta is the most splendid, the most fascinating, the most mysterious woman alive. She is the incarnation of beauty. I'm full of pride, crazy about her. I'm crazy about her in the way that mystics are crazy about God.

"Today I'm not going to the gallery" Marta says. "I have to go see a Dali exhibition in the Courtyard of Canova. Why don't you come too?"

"No Marta, I've seen more than enough Dali exhibits. They had one in the Courtyard of Canova last year as well. Now they're displaying him at the Galleria Colonna. I can't take any more of him".

"I don't love him all that much myself, but he's not as despicable as you make him out to be, if for no other reason than that he too was influenced by Giorgio de Chirico".

"He was a raving narcissist".

"All painters are narcissists. In his treatise *De pictura,* Leon Battista Alberti says that painting originated with Narcissus who sees his image reflected in the spring, or rather, as a self-portrait. Even Giorgio de Chirico was a narcissist, more so than the others perhaps. You just have to see and count his self-portraits. He painted himself more than Franz Hals, Rubens, Courbet and Picasso put together. And yet I love him just the same, in fact I adore him. De Chirico is immortal, whereas his distorted nephews will all die from self-love, and they won't even be transformed into flowers... For that matter, you too are a narcissist, without being a painter and without having Dali's talent".

75

"You're right, Marta, but I have no desire to see the same things all the time. If it were a de Chirico exhibit, I would gladly come".

"By the way, when will we go to Volos?"

"Next month. July will be here soon".

When we leave the restaurant, Piazza di Spagna is in a festive mood. The steps of Trinità dei Monti are resplendent with azaleas in bloom. The tourists stream through in growing waves, crowding around Bernini's Fountain.

Even Marta is in a festive mood.

"Why don't we go and see de Chirico's atelier from the window of your attic?" she asks. "I can go to the Dali exhibition later on".

"Yes, of course".

The small living room of my attic is flooded with light.

Marta leans out the window.

"De Chirico's atelier looks like an abandoned castle" she says, turning toward me with a seductive smile.

Before she does it herself, I undress her, undressing myself in turn.

"You look like Isis" I tell her.

"Adore me then".

I kneel down at her feet…

"Now it's your turn", I say, getting up.

She kneels down at my feet…

She gets up and leads me into the bedroom.

She has one orgasm after another, the first intense, the second extremely languorous…

She's like a tide that batters a defenseless object in successive waves and then stops suddenly, leaving it to drift…

Marta gets dressed and goes off to see the Dali exhibition, saying:

"If I have no other commitments, we can see each other at nine tonight at the Birreria Viennese".

"Agreed".

My ears are still ringing.

When she has an orgasm, Marta at first screams as though she's been mortally wounded, then lets out faint moans as though she were dying.

But she never says anything indecent or obscene, nor does she ask me to, like some of the women I've come across.

"I'm a big whore" a high school student from Rome used to say to me. She was studying with the Scolopi, a religious order who instilled in their students the idea that you have to achieve supremacy in everything in life.

"I want to hold it in my mouth the whole night" a Swiss girl that I met at Caffè Greco said. And yet her name was Theresa, like the saint of Lisieux, like the saint of Avila, like the saint of Gallura.

"For me the male organ is neutral: it has no master, it belongs to no one. I take it and that's that" a Parisian woman I met in the church of San Luigi dei Francesi said to me.

It is already twilight when I get up from the bed, exhausted. A light of antique gold is fading over the church of Trinità dei Monti and the abandoned castle.

The violinist is playing a Strauss waltz when we enter the Birreria Viennese around nine.

Marta greets him with a smile, saying:

"That's just what I needed. Strauss has a magical effect on me".

Perhaps in honor of Strauss, Marta orders an antipasto of Black Forest ham.

"For two" I tell the waiter.

"What shall we drink?" I ask her.

"Let's have beer".

I order two beers on tap.

When the waiter returns to ask if we want anything else, we order two more beers, but we finish them even before the entrees arrive. Then we order two more, leaving the entrees on our plates...

"Do you love me?" Marta suddenly asks me.

"Marta, haven't I shown you I do?"

"You have an odd way of having sex".

"You too, for that matter".

"For me sex is eros, Dionysian intoxication, divine madness, as Plato said".

"We'll fly high, tonight".

"If anything, you love my beauty, not me".

"But how can one distinguish your beauty from you?"

"They're two completely different things. I hate my beauty. I've already told you that it's brought me nothing but suffering. What do I have to do to make you understand, write a poem entitled 'Beauty, I hate you'?"

"What do you want me to tell you, that I love you but not your beauty?"

"It would be better, but it wouldn't be enough. I'd want to be loved even if I were ugly. I'd want you to love me even if I were a monster".

"But you are a monster: your beauty is monstrous".

"Stop being ironic, I beg you".

"Yes, your beauty is monstrous".

"Sappho says that only what you love is beautiful".

"You're beautiful in any case, whether you're loved or hated".

"But I could have been ugly. The body is accidental, transitory. Today it's resplendent, tomorrow hideous. Only the soul never changes. The soul pre-exists and survives the body. The body is nothing but the soul's enemy".

"Plato again?"

"Plato and Saint Augustine. I could have had a body completely different from this one. I could have been horrendous, as sooner or later I will be".

"But this is the body you have, and it's enviable".

"Why don't you talk about my soul?"

"Marta, I can't see your soul".

"You don't see anything".

"I don't know where it is".

"All you know is where my mouth is".

"Maybe you don't know either".

"You're an idiot!"

"Marta, please".

"You're a superficial man".

"Don't insult me, Marta, please".

"You're the one who's insulting me".

"I'm sorry".

"Sorry my ass!" she shouts, dousing me with the beer that's in her glass and stalking off...

I dry myself with the napkin, pay the bill and go after her.

She has already opened the door to 75 Via dei Greci when I catch up with her.

"Marta!" I say, but she slams the door in my face.

THE ENIGMA OF THE DEATH WISH

My father was possessed by a death wish.

More than once he tried to destroy himself and the entire family, which consisted of my mother and two other boys, both older than me. Twice he set fire to our house, a third time he set off a charge of TNT in the cellar. But the house was made of natural stone, and built on a rocky foundation; it was indestructible.

Near the house, between Via Cassia and Via Flaminia, was a railroad. A local, narrow-gauge train passed there several times each day. My brothers and I often went there to see it pass by. Beyond the railroad, stretched the land inherited by our father: land that extended as far as the eye could see, some parts cultivated and some in a natural state, at times opening onto grassy clearings and hillsides dotted with flowering plants, at times dipping into frightening depressions continuing into brush that obscured the horizon.

It was in that land that we ran wild in our adolescent years, often getting lost, falling from trees or from the precipices, and risking a fall into one of those infernal abysses.

Although he had a degree in agriculture, our father hated that land, but he adored an orchard that stood at the center of it and that he himself took care of: pears, apples, hazelnuts, cherries, almonds, peaches, mulberries, which almost all bloomed at the same time, quite suddenly. A long, endless sequence of colors: ivory white, soft pink, greenish gold, bright red, pale blue.

We anxiously awaited the end of winter to go and see them in their splendor.

But one fine day toward the end of spring, our father, out of the blue, had those wonderful plants brutally razed to the ground.

The orchard was transformed into a desert.

After those rudimentary attempts to destroy himself and the entire family, our father tried again in other ways. One day when he took us into the city center in his Land Rover, we almost ended up in the Tiber near the Duca d'Aosta bridge, all five of us.

My brothers said he was crazy, but for me he was an enigma.

Finally, having failed, my father resigned himself to dying alone.

Every night, drunk, he would go to meet death: he would fall asleep on the banks of the Tiber, on the side of the road used by heavy vehicles, or on the railroad escarpments.

More than once he was found by passersby, some of whom also took the trouble to bring him back home: he thanked them by heaping obscenities on them, saying they had no right to interfere in others' lives, that everyone was free to live or die as he wished.

When I began to realize that my father really wanted to die, I began to follow him.

I was ten years old.

I then discovered a number of things.

First, that there is a human scent just as there is an animal scent. I would sniff out my father's presence just as a hunting dog sniffs the presence of game, or a police dog the presence of a fugitive. I always ended up on the right track.

Second, that my father smelled my presence before I smelled his. I realized this clearly, many times.

81

Third, that he had a desperate need of proof of being loved.

When my father smelled my presence, he would play a pathetic game: if he was on the bank of the Tiber, he made as though to jump into the water; if he was on the side of the road used by heavy vehicles, he would stretch out in the middle of it; if he was on the railroad escarpment, he would lie down on the tracks. He would suddenly take himself into the danger zone, but then he made believe he didn't have the strength to pull back, falling like a corpse at the point from which I had removed him with great effort. More than once, when he was on the bank of the Tiber, he got up with a jump and tried to drag me with him into the whirlpools.

But after I had followed him for about six months, my father betrayed me.

It was an autumn night and there was a full moon which illuminated the grassy rises of the countryside, the outline of the hills, the railroad tracks and the river bed.

At one point I found myself at a place where the Tiber was overhung by a rocky cliff on which a dilapidated tower stood.

From that point I began to follow the course of the river carefully, walking against the current.

I walked a long way, searching from one bank to the other.

In a section where the water became shallow because of a shoal, I saw something entangled in the grass, near the shore.

The water was beating against it and then flowing back with an ominous gurgle.

I went nearer: he seemed to be sleeping, his head and shoulders above the water and the rest of his body submerged; his face was white and red, but around his mouth and eyes the skin was swollen and cracked, decomposing.

Even the wine-colored birthmark that used to shine on his forehead like an amethyst had dissolved.

I sat and waited near the river bank until it was daylight.

They say that all of us, some more than others, carry death, or the idea of death, within us from birth. But in many people, death or the idea of death can be seen in distinctive signs, in particular symptoms: it's as though these individuals bore invisible, though not imperceptible, stigmata on their hands, their face, their expression, or other parts of their body. Well, I have an eye which allows me to recognize these signs or symptoms, a sensitivity which permits me to perceive the presence of these stigmata. But rather than run from those people who bear the stigmata, I follow them, I'm attracted to them.

Up till now I have loved only my father.

No one else, not even my mother, who on the contrary, I couldn't stand: the fact that I'm in the world is due more to her than to my father, she's the one who carried me in her womb. An indigestion, a fall, some strong reaction would have sufficed for me never to have been born. But she never had any kind of indisposition, no accidents, in those nine months, despite the fact that she was subject to continual emotional upsets, even over nothing at all.

I loved my brothers even less: when I was a boy or teenager I saw them as my rivals, but then they became totally foreign to me.

The only happy moments of my childhood were spent with my father: I remember with nostalgic longing the days he brought me with him to the orchard (before he destroyed it), to the little churches or chapels of the surrounding area, to the inns on the hillsides all in bloom.

With the passing of time, the image of my father lying in the grass along the Tiber, rather than becoming blurred, has become ever more clear before my eyes.

It's like a sacred icon to me.

His face corroded by the water is imprinted upon my mind like that of Christ on the Shroud.

If I had not loved my father, I would not know what love is. After my father, not only have I never loved anyone else, man or woman, but I never wanted to be loved.

I detest all emotional display, all sentimental effusion, every form of gratuitous contact.

Nolite me tangere could be my motto.

With women, I prefer oral relations, if the partner prefers them in turn (I don't deny that that night in the doorway between Piazza di Spagna and Via Frattina, Diana submitted to it rather than wanted it, but that's the only time).

They say that oral relations humiliate women. What can be said about sodomy then, and those horrible positions in which the woman is taken from behind, hands and face down, ass up, like a monkey in the zoo? Michel Tournier says that you make love to someone out of love when the face inspires more desire than any other part of the body.

Oral relations have something poetic about them, something mystical.

Sandra would come to my place once a week, in the early afternoon, almost always at the same time. She was eighteen, tall, slender, with golden blond hair and blue eyes. She would enter on tiptoe, as if she were entering a church; her step was light, like that of a bird, her expression startled. She looked at objects as though she did not see them, as though no contact were established between her and them; she touched them as though they were unreal and as though she did not perceive their substance, sometimes letting them fall all of a sudden. She gave the impression that she hovered over herself in space, like a ghost. She spoke little or not at all, without ever raising her voice; you had to intuit her words from the movement of her lips, minimal movements, like one who is praying with the mind or heart more than the mouth. She loved Mozart, especially the *Requiem*, which I put on before she arrived.

She was a non-drinker, so I couldn't offer her anything nor drink anything with her to make the atmosphere less sterile. After a few minutes, I would make myself comfortable on the sofa, and she would approach and kneel down at my feet: she reached out and drew back her arms as though they were wings, she moved her hands and fingers as though touching a stringed instrument, she raised and lowered her head like a swan. She performed the ritual with the purity of a nurse in an operating room, but at the same time with passion, a cold passion, like that of a liturgical mystery. This was, so to speak, agape or spiritual love.

When the rite was complete, she got up and left, without breathing, on tiptoe, as she had come.

I never saw her naked, nor did I know if she went to other houses, or other churches, on the other days of the week.

Even Sister Edvige, who I went to twice a week for my injections, followed a more or less unchanging ritual. She would lead me silently into a small, faintly lit chapel, invite me with a nod to sit on a small bench, and kneel down at my feet with a look full of tenderness.

I don't know if she experienced pleasure or not, but I would think not.

For her it was a pious act.

Anna Maria gave me the feeling that she might suddenly bite into it, and tear it to shreds.

Alessandra at the moment of climax sees herself in the role of Judith who decapitates Holofernes in his sleep.

85

Giulia seems determined to devour it each time; maybe she's seen Oshima's *Realm of the Senses* on TV.

Barbara has an orgasm before coming to my place, by mentally envisioning the scene. It's a form of eroticism that is imaginary, yet real, similar to the eroticism of dreams but less fleeting.

According to what they say, the male's semen cures illnesses, especially tuberculosis, and restores the skin by making infections, eczema or acne disappear.

"Come on my face" a classmate at school used to tell me. Another girl friend from that time would take it in her hands and spread it on her face. They were both fifteen years old. Perhaps their aesthetic science was inherited from their mothers.

Up till now there were only two women who wanted nothing to do with it. The first was Turkish, a Moslem: she told me that her religious, or hygienic-religious, convictions did not allow it. The second was Brazilian, a Hindu: she told me that that sexual practice was an outrage to Eros, which is sacred, divine, a spiritual passion.

Marta has the same ideas as the Brazilian girl.
But if her body is accidental, and could be different than it is – today splendid and tomorrow decrepit – why does she use it in such an egotistical way? It's with her body that she assails me, more than with her soul. It's not as if she says: "Here's my despicable body: you're free to do what you want with it". No. She rules over it herself, despotically. Like my father, Marta too, whether she was conceived with or without love, whether or not she has a desperate need to feel loved, is an enigma for me.

THE MYSTERY OF THE FEMALE MOUTH

"All you know is where my mouth is" Marta said to me.

It's true: the first thing I look at in a woman is her mouth. My eyes go immediately to the mouth. For me the mouth is the most precious element of a woman's face; I might almost say that for me the mouth is everything. They say that the eyes are the mirror of the soul. But it's the mouth, if anything, which is the mirror of the soul. Even the author of the *Song of Songs* gives great importance to the mouth.

Your lips are like a scarlet ribbon;
desirable is your mouth…

Your lips drip sweetness as the honeycomb, my bride;
milk and honey are within your mouth…

Your lips are roses
Soft with resinous myrrh…

I know very well that King Solomon (or whoever wrote for him, probably a Helenized Hebrew poet) is referring to kisses.

Let me drink the kisses of your mouth…

But my reluctance to kissing is very strong. For me the kisses of the female mouth have mainly one object. When I read the verse of the *Song*: "His fruit is sweet in my mouth", I think only of him.

However, I don't think about the female mouth the same way that the Parisian woman I met in the church of San

Luigi dei Francesi thinks about the male organ. For me the female mouth is not neutral, belonging to no one. It's the most sensitive part of a woman's face, revealing and expressing her personality.

When I was seventeen or eighteen, I only had to look at a woman's mouth to get an idea of her personality, and depending on the idea I formed from it, I felt attracted or not to the mouth itself and to the woman to whom it belonged. But today it's much more difficult for me to form an idea from a mouth. Nowadays the mouths of both mature women and young or very young women are to a great extent artificial: false, obscene mollusks, which swell and deflate like medusas. The other night I abandoned an ex-classmate from university, who was celebrating his birthday in a Rome discotheque, after only ten minutes: almost all of the women present had identical mouths, evidently contrived by the same plastic surgeon. To find a mouth in its natural state is a rarity today. Not even I, who have a certain familiarity with female mouths, am able to tell them apart them anymore. Mouths which revealed and expressed personalities that seemed interesting to me, disgust me in practice, while other mouths, anything but interesting in appearance, can send me into delirium.

The female mouth is a mystery.

Nonetheless, whether or not I make a mistake, it is unlikely that I would have contact with a mouth that makes me predict a personality which holds little interest.

I did it only once, but passively, almost against my will.

It was the mouth of a Swedish film actress who had come to me to ask me to publish her photos. Her mouth appeared unpleasant from the start, just as she herself appeared unpleasant to me. But the photos were interesting, and I told her that I would publish several of them. Perhaps out of emotion, or for some other obscure reason, she confided to me about some intimate matters. Her lover demanded oral services while he stretched out on the couch and watched this or that television program, without speaking, without ever looking at her.

"Here, I'll show you how the scene is played" she said; "turn on the television and stretch out in this armchair".

I turned on the television and stretched out in the armchair.

She knelt down at my feet and performed the scene, realistically, in its entirety.

I got up feeling nauseous.

"I'll never publish her photos" I told myself. But she added: "He demands my oral services even while he is sitting at his desk reading or writing. He loves me to slip stealthily under the desk, like a cat".

I refrained from asking her why she didn't rebel, but I avoided sitting at the desk until she went away.

Although I am unable to see the female mouth except in the context of the face, mentally or abstractly I can also see it isolated from all the rest, like a rose detached from its stem, branches and leaves. In either case, however, I do not exclude the hair, especially if it is red or tawny, long and flowing: in the rhythmic movement of the mouth in action, the hair plays a choreographic role, so to speak. Sometimes, if the partner has the gift of irony, I make use of transparent mirrors: the triplication of our images has a grotesque, exhilarating effect. Not to accompany the *Requiem*, of course; if anything, *Così fan tutte*...

The rose detached from its stem, branches and leaves fascinates me, more than any other image.

I've cut out dozens of female mouths, belonging to important women from history, literature, art, mythology and above all, current news. The idea came to me from the *Sheherazades* and the mouth-vulvas of Magritte, as well as from the op artists who painted mouths on the stomachs of their models. I repainted some of the mouths – such as those of the Madonnas of Giovanni Bellini, Raphael and

Leonardo, of Rubens' ladies, of Lucas Cranach the Elder's Venuses, of El Greco's *Lady with the Ermine*, of Dante Gabriele Rossetti's women – on big sheets of white paper and made albums from them.

I now have an extensive collection, which I look at continually, especially in the hours of the night when, after yet another tussle with Marta, I need to relax a bit before going to bed.

My favorite mouths? They belonged, or belong, to the most diverse women. I'll cite some of them, at random:

Nefertiti, Cleopatra, Saint Teresa of Avila, Paolina Bonaparte, Galina Ulanova, Jean Harlow, Francesca Bertini, Ava Gardner, Michèle Morgan, Liv Ullman, Julia Roberts, Melanie Griffith, Nicole Kidman...

Then there are those that I've rejected because I was convinced, after more careful examination, that there was nothing exciting or mysterious about them, but above all because they had been – or have been – recreated one or more times. For these too I'll cite the first names that come to mind:

Eleonora Duse, Isadora Duncan, Marlene Dietrich, Liz Taylor, Sophia Loren, Jeanne Moreau, Anita Ekberg, Catherine Deneuve, Madonna, Claudia Schiffer...

The mouth I love the most is that of Dante Gabriele Rossetti's Beatrice, also because it makes me think of Marta's mouth. In second place is that of Magritte's Anne-Marie Crowet, especially the version in which her long yellow-gold hair appears in full.

I cut out Beatrice's mouth, had it framed against a gold background, and hung it on the wall in front of my bed.

Now I have to face a more subtle question: the role of the mouth in relation to the beauty of a woman's face.

Marta quoted Dürer: "I don't know what beauty is". But Marta is personally involved in the question; she lacks the necessary detachment, and resorts to citations which are to her advantage. Besides, Dürer suffered from depression, and was unable to see the beauty around him; not even his Madonnas glow with great beauty.

So as not to have Marta, who took a course in ancient philosophy at the French Academy, continue to catch me unprepared by citing Plato or Saint Augustine, the other night I read as much as I could of the Greek philosopher and the bishop of Hippo.

I read Plato's *Symposium* and *Phaedo*, or rather the two dialogues on Eros, which is to say on beauty and beauty itself. But I also reread them, because on the first reading they made a negative impression on me. The participants at the symposium were all a bit feeble-minded: some hung over from the day before, some getting drunk now, some who would be hung over before the symposium ended. Toward the end they all collapsed except Socrates, who was drinking as well, but who could hold his liquor. In addition, they all seemed a little like gays or queers in a frenzy, anxious to get a seat next to Socrates and obtain his favors, wagging their tail around the Master like monkeys drunk on gin or wasted on coke.

Before relating what I understood (or what I think I understood), I must confess that reading the first pages of the *Symposium* I experienced a small jolt. It happened when Pausanias, the lover of Agathon, who is in turn the lover of Socrates, says that an action – therefore even a sexual or erotic action – is not beautiful or ugly in itself, but according to how it is performed.

"That's just what I told Marta" I thought.

I therefore went looking for the places where Plato speaks of beauty and beauty itself.

There are two passages in which he speaks of it, relating what Socrates says about it, the latter relaying what he was told by Diotima of Mantinea, a prophetess experienced in the "mysteries of beauty".

"What a muddle this *Symposium* is!" I said to myself. "A

follower and admirer of Socrates, Apollodorus, reports a conversation on Eros which took place 'many years earlier' and which had been reported to him by another follower and admirer of Socrates, Aristodemos, to whom it had probably been reported by another follower and admirer of Socrates".

In any case, in the first passage Socrates says that Beauty is Moira (one of the fates, the goddess of birth and death) and Eilithyia (the goddess who presides over childbirth and generation): "Therefore, when the pregnant comes near to a beautiful thing it becomes gracious, and being delighted it is poured out and begets and procreates", while "when it comes near to an ugly thing, it becomes gloomy and grieved and rolls itself up and is repelled and shrinks back and does not procreate, but holds back the conception and is in a bad way".[10]

After having read this drivel, I still didn't know what beauty and ugliness are, what beauty itself is and what ugliness itself is. Nor did I understand it when Socrates reports, in the second passage, that beauty itself is genuine, pure, sincere, and unvarying, and that those who are able to contemplate it become immortal.

The only thing I was able to draw from it is that beauty itself is immortal, or rather, one of the Ideas of the ultra-sensory world, and that beauty is specifically a property of the soul, which is also immortal, while physical beauty is short-lived, ephemeral, like the body itself.

"Marta is right about that" I told myself.

I had to read the discourse of Eryximachos to learn that beauty is harmony of the parts and ugliness disharmony of the parts, that beauty is order, ugliness disorder.

But I still didn't know what the so-called "science of beauty" is.

"Maybe not even Socrates and Plato know" I said to myself.

But let's proceed in order, or rather in beauty.

The banquet was given by Agathon, a thirty year old gay dramatist who is celebrating his victory in a tragedy competition. Those taking part are Phaidros, Pausanias, Aristophanes, Socrates, Alcibiades, and others. They take turns speaking, at ever greater length (Aristophanes skips his turn because he has hiccups and will speak later on), going on and on. An oratorical tournament that would make you expire.

Phaidros, a descendent of Athenian high society and also one of Socrates' lovers, takes the floor first. He says that there is no god more ancient, venerable and benevolent than Eros: he is so portentous that if, hypothetically, a state or an army were composed exclusively of lovers and beloved, the state would be governed splendidly and the army would fight magnificently (that the states, nations and countries would be governed splendidly, or in any case much better than they are today, is more than probable, in fact, it's a sure thing; but it's rather doubtful that armies made up of gay lovers, perhaps with heads girded with ivy, violets and ribbons like Agathon, would fight magnificently).

Aristophanes, the comedic playwright who had held Socrates up to derision in his *Clouds*, is the only one who does not sing the praises of gay love; on the contrary he does not hesitate to tease Pausanias and Agathon. On top of that, he gives a very entertaining talk on the myth of the hermaphrodite, though it too is incoherent and wordy.

"At first there were three sexes, not two as at present, male and female, but also a third having both together. Next, the shape of man was quite round, back and ribs passing about it in a circle; and he had four arms and an equal number of legs, and two faces on a round neck, exactly alike; there was one head with these two opposite faces, and four ears, and two privy members…"[11]

"The double sexes have come back into style" I thought,

"but today, thanks to surgery, you can eliminate one or the other and become male or female as it suits you".

Socrates then interrupts and after a long preamble, proclaims that Eros is a great demon, half divine and half human, something between immortal and mortal: "First, he is always poor; and far from being tender and beautiful, as most people think, he is hard and rough and unshod and homeless, always lying on the ground, with no bedding, sleeping in doorways and in the streets in the open air, having his mother's nature, always dwelling with want. But from his father again he has designs upon beautiful and good things, being brave and go-ahead and high-strung, a mighty hunter, always weaving devices, and a successful coveter of wisdom, a philosopher all his days, a great wizard and sorcerer and sophist"[12] (it is superfluous to note that Socrates has merely traced his own portrait, that is, the portrait of an incomparable smart ass, one of the great faggots of history).

But Socrates stages the most amazing *coup de théatre* in Phaedra: the same Eros who the participants of the Symposium had proclaimed to be just, temperate, balanced, possessed of great self-control, and supremely Olympic, gives himself up to passion, folly, delirium, unbridled Dionysian intoxication, and orgiastic fury, transforming himself into a divine sexual maniac, pedophile, vampire, Dracula, Nosferatu, Frankenstein...

thing to add: when I imagine Diotima of Mantinea who unveils the "mysteries of beauty" to Socrates, I am reminded of a shrew, a Great Whore, a kind of forerunner of Fellini's Saraghina.

As for Saint Augustine, I reread the main parts of the *Confessions* and read *Beauty,* an essay in *De pulchro et de apto,* the little book that the future saint had written when he was twenty seven, and which had already been lost in his own time.

What does Augustine, the two-faced Janus, think about beauty, beauty itself, and Eros?

The pagan Augustine thinks what Plato and Plotinus thought: true beauty is beauty of the spirit or of the soul; beauty itself is Plato's Idea and Plotinus' One; Eros is the desire for beauty. And physical or corporeal beauty? It's the correct proportion of the parts, together with a certain loveliness of complexion.

The Christian Augustine identifies Plato's Idea and Plotinus' One with God, the Father of beauty, Beauty of all Beauties, converts the Eros of Plato and Plotinus into agape or caritas (the virtue through which one approaches the contemplation of Absolute Beauty), and proclaims that Christ is the most beautiful among the sons of man.

"It's not as though Saint Augustine's thinking shines with overwhelming originality" I said to myself.

But what I couldn't swallow was the idea that the face or the body, to be beautiful, had to possess "the elegance of complexion", as Agathon says, or "the grace of coloring", as Plotinus says, or "a certain loveliness of complexion" as Augustine says.

What about those who are pallid? What about men and women who in every age have been proclaimed beautiful despite the pallor of their faces or bodies? What about Saint Catherine of Siena and Saint Teresa of Avila, Sarah Bernhardt and Eleonora Duse, Francesca Bertini and Valentina Cortese, who were (or are) all pallid, extremely pale. What about Greta Garbo, who embodied, so to speak, pallor itself, absolute pallor? Above all, what about Sappho, who said of herself: "I turn paler than dry grass"? How could Sappho have been ugly if Plato himself says in the *Symposium* that she was beautiful? Was the greatest poetess of antiquity rosy and beautiful, or pallid and ugly?

I was asking myself these questions when I fell asleep toward five in the morning.

BEAUTY IS A DIABOLICAL ILLUSION

Marta bombarded me with phone calls, both during the day and at night, but I resisted her assault. Last night, however, a little after seven thirty, she came to the editorial office unexpectedly, entering my office without being announced.

"Forgive me, I wanted to surprise you. I'm sorry about the other night" she said, with an alluring smile.

I was not able to go on resisting her (to tell the truth, I felt a strong emotion after our not having seen each other for a good five days).

When we go down to Via del Babuino and she walks along in the middle of the street a couple of meters in front of me, I experience a kind of visual shock. It's as though I were just seeing her that moment, as though she hadn't come to the editorial office and we hadn't come down together, as though her image had been erased from my retina in the five days that we hadn't seen each other. Her figure cancels every other presence, creating an empty space in which she stands out. She's the same, and yet there's always something surprisingly new about her. It's difficult to say what it is, but it renders her beauty more enigmatic, her natural elegance more portentous.

"Why don't we go to a new place for supper?" she asks me.

"Have you ever eaten at the restaurant in the Hotel d'Inghilterra?"

"No, I've been to the bar once or twice, but never to the restaurant".

"Do you want to try it?"
"Let's go".

"I started writing the poem tonight " she says, while we're having a whisky at the bar.
"The poem about beauty?"
"Exactly, but I only wrote about a dozen lines".
"Did you bring them with you?"
"No. I prefer finishing it before having you read it".
"What do you say in those first lines?"
"That beauty is a diabolical illusion".
"I'm eager to read it".

As we drink our whisky, I notice that there are cuts on her hands; there are light traces of dried blood.
"This afternoon we hung a new exhibit, at least a hundred and fifteen canvases" she says, aware that I am looking at her hands.
"Who's being shown?"
" Mario Schifano".
"Oh, yes, I received an invitation but I couldn't go to the preview".
"Couldn't, or didn't want to?"
"I wasn't able to. One of his former assistants had even called me, asking me to write something about it in "Ulysses 3000" or the "New Tribune".
"It's the first exhibition arranged for him after his death. You have to come and see it".
"I'll come".
"I was overcome by an immense sadness while I was hanging his paintings".
"Are there new paintings?"
"He always tried to do new work, up until the end, but he painted too much, and in too much of a rush, as though he had a premonition that the end was near. The dealers would not leave him in peace. And yet some of his

97

last paintings, such as *War Crimes Trial, Deus, San Francisco, Uno mas,* are very beautiful. What is most striking about them is the painter's eye: an eye that is able to catch the fleeting moment and fix it on the canvas. His eye was like a laser. I know very well that the choice of images and colors takes place in the brain and not in the retina, as the Impressionists believed, but his eye was internal, mental, or transmental…"

I want to ask her if Schifano too wasn't a "nephew" of de Chirico, but she interrupts me:

"He was a new and original painter".

"I'll come soon".

"But all you'll see are the last bursts of a talent in extinction. He had been destroyed. They arrested him many times, just because he used drugs a little; they imprisoned him, actually locked him up in an asylum, as though he were an insane criminal. The only reason he didn't collapse sooner was because he was 'crucified to a horseshoe', as he himself used to say with his own desperate attempt at humor".

"I'm anxious to see the show. I'll come tomorrow morning".

The restaurant at the Hotel d'Inghilterra is already crowded. For the most part they are men, Italians and foreigners, but there is also a party of Russians, who noisily break the silence of that discreet atmosphere.

Marta's entrance rouses general attention.

The eyes of those in the room follow her every movement with an insistence that is unpleasant, to say the least. They continue to look at her even after she has sat down in front of me, at a table in a corner of the room which I had asked for when we arrived.

"I want something French" Marta says to the waiter.

The waiter hands us the menus.

"A plate of escargots and an entrecote avec champignons" Marta tells him.

"Grilled steak for me" I tell him.

She would like a bottle of Chateauneuf du pape, but they don't have any, so she orders a bottle of Chablis to start, then a bottle of Beaujolais.

"The other night I read some books on a subject that interests you" I say.

"Which books?"

"Plato's *Symposium* and *Phaedo*, and an essay on what Saint Augustine thinks about beauty, which is in fact entitled *Beauty*. I also reread the *Confessions* of Saint Augustine.

"Now I have to be on guard".

"Now you're the one being ironic".

"Do you want to give me a hard time?"

"I wouldn't dare".

"You're a hypocrite".

"Marta, please".

"If you reread the *Confessions*, you'd realize that what Saint Augustine says about beauty is mere nonsense. He says that objects or persons attract us because of their propriety and grace, because if they didn't have them, they wouldn't attract us. But that's a tautology, besides being nonsense. He says that beauty is loved for itself, while ugliness is unloved for itself. He had taken these ideas from Plato and Plotinus, but he was a racist just like them. They created a radical distinction between the beautiful and the ugly, condemning the ugly to eternal unhappiness. I'll tell you, I prefer ugliness, even the most monstrous ugliness, to their beauty".

"At that time no one thought that ugliness could have a certain fascination".

"Great discovery! But that's not the point. We have to destroy the criteria which have been used to determine what is beautiful and what is ugly. Those criteria have no basis. Besides, of what use is it to me to be considered beautiful by others if I don't see myself that way? Or most of all, if I don't feel beautiful?"

99

"You're right, Marta".

"When you tell me I'm right, you irritate me more than when you act ironic or tell me you don't agree with me".

"I'm sorry... In any case, you said that for Saint Augustine the body is the enemy of the soul, while Saint Augustine says that corporeal beauty is a reflection of divine beauty".

"You haven't understood a thing. In the *Confessions*, Saint Augustine says that when he was in love with earthly beauty he was walking toward the abyss. If corporeal beauty were a reflection of divine beauty, why was he walking toward the abyss?"

"Because when he was in love with earthly beauty he had not yet discovered the beauty of God, that is, he had not yet converted".

"His conversion has never convinced me. I read the *Confessions* for the first time in Paris, in French, but even at that time they raised tremendous doubts in me. It's the book of a narcissist: 'Me, me, me, *my* God, *my* God, *my* God'... It seems as though God is something that belongs only to him, his own personal hunting ground, as though God were speaking exclusively to him... He goes so far as to say that he had a terrible childhood, but he had no idea of what a terrible childhood is..."

"Marta, please don't raise your voice".

"I couldn't care less about these idiots who are listening to us!"

"Me either, but I don't think they want to hear a lecture about Saint Augustine".

"I've had to put up with their lascivious eyes all this time".

"Marta, I simply asked you not to raise your voice".

"What sends me into a rage is the idea Saint Augustine had about women. From the very first pages of the *Confessions*, as he talks about this or that woman, he doesn't hesitate to call them 'donnicciole', little women. He behaved horribly toward the Unnamed one. Although he had a son by her, he abandoned her to marry a woman who was respectable, and rich to boot. The Unnamed was made to go away so as not to disturb the wedding. She went to Africa vowing never to be with anyone else, while he quickly took a new lover and then got engaged to a woman who 'everybody liked', as he says in the book, despite the fact that she was barely twelve years old".

"Marta, we were talking about beauty".

"I'll tell you what beauty is: beauty is horrifying!"

She gets up with a jolt, hurls her glass on the parquet, in the direction of the few remaining diners, and grabs her purse:

"I'm fed up with you and all these shit heads!" she shouts, leaving like a shot.

The waiters hurry to pick up the pieces of glass, under the disconcerted eyes of the bystanders.

The room empties as though by magic.
I leave as well.

I go to Le diable au corps.

The dance floor is in full swing.

I sit at the bar, on the raised platform, from which I can observe the scene.

Diana isn't there, but Marta is.

She's dancing with one of the frenzied adolescents: tall, lean, long, teased black hair, earrings, tattoos.

All of a sudden she pulls him close and kisses him passionately on the mouth, at the same time simulating the sex act while moving to the beat of the rock music. Then she takes him by the arm and leaves with him.

I can't say if she saw me, but I think she did.

She may not have Diana's radar, but she has hypersensitive receptors.

THE JAPANESE WOMAN WITH A MOUTH
OF RUBY RED

"The hell with Marta" I tell myself as soon as I wake up.

It's the first thought of the day.

I get dressed and go to Babington's, where I reward myself with a magnificent breakfast: bacon and eggs, grapefruit juice, and blueberries. Then I take a stroll around the *centro*, along the sunny streets, and finally I land in the editorial office.

I glance at the newspapers stopping at interesting items, such as the one which says that some lions have escaped from the zoo and are roaming around the Circus Maximus, where once upon a time their ancestors dismembered the Christians ("they're waiting there for the Holy Year pilgrims" the reporter writes maliciously). Afterwards I work a little, but I have no real desire to so I go to lunch at Casina Valadier, a lovely restaurant near the Pincio at the entrance to Villa Borghese on the Villa Medici side.

I order an aperitif, and while waiting for the waiter to bring it, I look at the panorama.

The basilica of Saint Peter's appears dazzling in the sky, like a Taj Mahal. The gold of the domes reflects the radiant light of the noonday sun, and the horizon line vanishes into a bluish violet against the distant mountains.

On the table next to me is a Japanese woman.

I greet her with a bow.

She gives me an alluring smile.
I get up and sit at her table.

She's wearing a black suit with a white blouse and red shoes, a string of white pearls around her neck.

"Are you a model, a photographer's model?"
"You're mistaken".
"What do you do?"
"I paint".
"Why type of painting do you do?"
"Sacred art".
"Where did you study?"
"I used to draw when I was a teenager in Tokyo, but I went to the Academie des Beaux Arts in Paris, and after that I came to Italy".
"Where and how did you learn your excellent Italian?"
"When I settled in Rome, I took a course at the 'Dante Alighieri', but I already knew Italian pretty well. I learned it wandering around Italy studying sacred art. I adore Byzantine Madonnas, the Madonnas of Italian primitive painters, of the Italian artists of the Fifteenth-Sixteenth century".
"I've never been so taken in before" I tell her.
"Don't worry about it".
"I should have noticed that you have the hands of an artist".
"Thank you so much. What do you do?"
"I'm the editor-in-chief of a new cultural magazine, 'Ulysses 3000', and I write literary and artistic reviews for the Rome daily 'The New Tribune'".
"I too would never have imagined that you were a writer" she says with an ironic smile.
"Now we're even" I reply, smiling at her.
"What's your name, if I may ask?"
"Andrea Boldini".
"I know your signature".

I observe her as we eat and drink, while pretending to be interested in other things.

She has an asymmetrical face, exceedingly remarkable: a broad forehead, long black hair, high cheekbones, delicate, luminous skin, dark brown almond-shaped eyes. The wide, thin mouth of ruby red splits the space between the nose and chin like a double-edged, red-hot blade. The arms and hands are long, with nails that seem like talons, painted red. Her smile is open one moment, barely there the next, difficult to decipher.

"I want to go to the Galleria Borghese", she says after we've had coffee. "I want to go back and see a Madonna of Giovanni Bellini, the *Madonna and child* of 1510. She's so pure that every time I see her I feel an impulse to kneel down. Would you like to come with me?"

"Gladly".

"You're very kind".

"Are you Christian, Catholic?"

"No, I'm a Shintoist, but I love the purity of Italian sacred art".

We reach the Galleria Borghese and climb the steps.

She very quickly finds the Madonna of Giovanni Bellini.

Her gaze lights up.

She stays there for several minutes; she appears to be in a trance.

"Please don't get on your knees" I want to say to her; but she interrupts my thoughts:

"I also like the *Venus* of Lucas Cranach the Elder very much. It's in gallery X, in the right hand corner, just in front of Braccianino's *Venus*, with its enormous cubed breasts, which I don't like at all".

"Let's go see it".

We see the *Venus* of Lucas Cranach the Elder, make a quick tour of the other galleries, and leave.

"Now I'll take you to see the Lake House" I tell her. "The landscape surrounding it is very romantic. There are even wild camellias".

"I love the almond trees in bloom. In Tokyo, when spring came, I would go to the main cemetery almost every day to see them flower".

"I'm sorry, here the almond trees are finished blooming by now".

We take a stroll around the lake.

"I often go to the Vatican Museum; I have a special pass so I can go in whenever I want to" she says. "The first time I went there I also visited the apartments of the Borgias. They made an enormous impression on me. Since then I've visited five or six times. Pope Alessandro, Valentino, Lucrezia, what characters!

Pope Borgia, Pope Borgia
Instead of saying Mass
He prepares an orgy

they used to say about that Pope".

"Rome must have been a demoniacal city at that time".

"Even now, for that matter".

"The Borgias were great experts when it came to poisons".

"Especially a poison which they extracted from a tree that doesn't exist anymore. It was a poison that had no antidote. But now in Rome they extract many other poisons ".

"Rome is one of a kind".

"Where is your studio?" I ask her, as we cross the Viale delle Magnolie.

"In Via del Babuino, in a building where Poussin had his studio".

105

"An ambitious choice".

"No, no, I found it through a friend, I didn't know that Poussin had had his studio in that building. I would be pleased if you could come and see my paintings some day".

"If you'd like, I could even come right now".

"You're infinitely kind".

I had never seen a studio so precious, so unusual.

Lofts, stairs, ladders, chests decorated in silver, cabinets inlaid with gold, enameled caskets…

On the easel is a canvas on which she is in the process of drawing a Madonna, still in its early stages.

"It's the Madonna of Giovanni Bellini" she says. "I've tried to re-do it several times now, but it's never come out right. This time I hope to succeed".

All around are her paintings: Madonnas, angels, saints, virgins, crucifixes, cupids; various sacred objects, books on sacred art, with illuminated covers.

"Do you like my paintings?" she asks me, indicating to some of them.

"They're interesting…"

"Which do you like the most?"

"The Madonnas, but you…"

"Tell me, tell me…"

"One feels too strongly the presence of the models that inspire you… You should free yourself from these influences, try to achieve a more personal style".

"That's what I'm striving to do… With your help perhaps I could achieve it more quickly".

"I can only give you suggestions, and modest suggestions at that. I'm not an expert in sacred art".

"I have a lot of trust in your judgment, in your help".

"Thank you, I'll try to help you, though I don't know how".
"Possibly you could write something about me".
"Yes, of course".

"Come, I want to show you some things I've never shown to anyone" she says, indicating one of the lofts and inviting me to follow her up.

She opens a chest and takes out a small canvas:
"It's a Madonna from the school of Pietro Perugino" she says, holding it before me.
"It's enchanting".
She opens the chest again, replaces the canvas and takes out a drawing.
"It's by a student of Raphael" she says.
"It's wonderful".
"Don't think they're fake" she adds, putting the drawing back in the chest.
"I'm not an expert in sacred art, as I told you, but I have no reason to think they're fake".

"Now I'll show you something else" she says, opening a casket: in it is a papal ring with an amethyst, in a case lined in white velvet.
"I've never shown these things to anyone, but I have a strong feeling that I can trust you" she says, closing the casket and inviting me to climb down from the loft.
As I go down, I notice on a shelf a silver chalice and a nickel-plated holy water sprinkler.

"Would you like tea?"
"Yes, thank you".
"Please take off your shoes" she says, handing me a pair of slippers, and slipping on a pair herself.
"Come" she adds, opening a small door on the right, at the back of the studio.

107

She leads me into a small room, papered entirely in Japanese prints and lithographs, the floor covered by a large mat; the room contains a sofa-bed and a corner cooking unit.

"This is where I recover my identity, my origins" she says.

"Were you born in Tokyo?"

"No, I was born in Tembun, the birthplace of Kano Eitoku, the great sixteenth century painter. I come from an ancient family of samurais. But my parents moved to Tokyo when I was ten. The desire to devote myself to painting was born in me through studying the works of Kano Eitoku at home".

"Were the prints and lithographs on the wall done by Kano Eitoku?"

"Yes. He's the Japanese painter that I love the most".

"But how did you come to have a love for Italian painting?"

"When I was twelve years old my father, who had opened a gallery of ancient art in Tokyo, took me with him on a trip to Europe. We visited Amsterdam, Paris, London, but especially the great cities of Italian art, Venice, Florence, Rome..."

She takes off her jacket and sets the tray with the tea down on the mat.

"Take your jacket off too, if you'd like".

I take off my jacket.

She kneels down and sits on the soles of her feet.

Her skirt rides up; I glimpse at the black halo of her sex.

"Do as I'm doing".

I kneel down and sit like her, facing her.

As she pours the tea, her breasts emerge from her blouse which she has unbuttoned.

"This is how they used to have tea once upon a time in Japan" she says, having closed the distance between us,

108

bending her head down from time to time and brushing against me with her mouth.

"I'm glad to have met you" she says.
"I'm even more glad".

Behind a curtain I see a built-in chest of drawers. A golden key shines on each draw and beneath each key black writing, in Japanese, stands out.
"I keep the pigments for painting in those drawers" she says, having noticed me looking at them.
But they seem like funeral urns to me.
There is the vague odor of a crematorium in the air.

"The ceremony is over" she says, getting up.
Seen from below, her body seems to have tentacles, but I can still feel the fire of her mouth on me.
I too get up and follow her into the studio.

"Excuse me, I don't mean to be indiscreet, but how did the things you showed me come into your possession?"
"I have many friends in the Vatican".
"But those things are precious, rare".
"I'm kind to them".
"I understand, but kindness perhaps isn't enough to obtain such gifts".
"I make them happy".
"But they're men dedicated to God and the Church, they should already be happy".
"You're pretending not to understand".
"Explain it to me, then".
"It's a secret" she says, with an ambiguous smile, adding: "Thank you for coming, I hope to see you again".
"Me too".

The secret was in her red-hot blade.

NEC SINE TE NEC TECUM VIVERE POSSUM

I spent part of last night with Ovid.

For some time the phrase *Nec sine te nec tecum vivere possum* was going around in my head, but I couldn't remember where I read it nor who had written it. It seemed to me that that phrase reflected my relationship with Marta.

Last night I solved the problem.

The phrase is found in the Latin poet's *Loves*.

It's in paragraph XI of the third Book, in the lines of the final section:

> *A fugitive from your vices, I'm lured back by your beauty:*
> *Your morals turn me off, your body on.*
> *So I can live neither with nor without you, I don't seem*
> *To know my own mind. I wish you were*
> *Either less beautiful or more faithful: such a good figure*
> *Doesn't go with your bad ways.*[13]

At first I said, with amazement: "Yes, Ovid's relationship with that woman is surprisingly similar to my relationship with Marta". But then I reread paragraph XI in its entirety, all 42 verses, and little by little my amazement diminished.

It's not known if Ovid was referring to his Corinna, to another one of his lovers, or to one of his wives. Probably he was referring to another one of his lovers. But although he tells her that he was behaving toward her not only like a custodian and companion, but also like a husband, in reality they were not living together. She lived alone, and did not hesitate to receive other men in her home, betraying and humiliating him. He himself admits it, not without shame: "A tardy access of horn...I was forced to watch your lover/Lurch home exhausted, done in!/Yet even this hurt less than *him* seeing *me*."[14] The poet had a love-hate relationship with that woman: "The facts demand censure, the face begs for love – and gets it"[15] he tells her. Although he couldn't live either with her or without her, he still preferred to live with her rather than without her.

Love versus hate – but love, I think, will win.
I'll hate if I can. If not I'll play the reluctant lover:
No ox loves the yoke – he's just stuck with what he hates.[16]

"There are certainly similarities" I told myself. "That woman was beautiful, too beautiful, Marta is beautiful, too beautiful; Ovid would have liked her to be less beautiful, perhaps I too would like Marta to be less beautiful; that woman was wicked and did things that deserved hatred, I don't know if Marta is wicked or does things that deserve hatred, but she acts in a way that bewilders me, that leaves me very agitated; that woman betrayed him, Marta betrays me; Ovid preferred to live with her rather than without her, I prefer to live with Marta rather than without Marta. Every time Marta did something upsetting, I told myself: 'I don't want to see her anymore', but each time I found I had an even stronger desire to see her..."

"But the differences" I continued to tell myself "are greater than the similarities. Ovid was jealous of his woman, I'm not jealous of Marta; Ovid suffered because she betrayed him, I'm not suffering because she betrays me; Ovid felt humiliated by having seen the man with whom she was betraying him leave his lover's house, and even more so by having been seen by him, I didn't feel at all humiliated by having seen the man with whom Marta was betraying me (I'm not aware if he knew that Marta is my lover, but even if it were so I would not have felt humiliated); Ovid had a love-hate relationship with that woman, I have never hated Marta, nor do I hate her, at least not on a conscious level. I don't know if the victor in our case will be love, but I'm certain it won't be hate, also because, still on a conscious level, I don't know what hatred is... Maybe I made a huge mistake. Marta has nothing in common with that woman, and I have nothing in common with Ovid. They were two useless lovers, two miserable losers. I wasted my time and lost sleep pointlessly" I finally told myself.

I've already said that I've never loved anyone, just as I have never been loved by anyone, or rather, that I never wanted to love, much less be loved. I don't know what being in love means, nor what it means to be the object of someone's falling in love. I don't even know what jealousy, betrayal, and the suffering due to jealousy and betrayal are; they're things I've read about in books, or that others have told me about, but I've never experienced them.

My relationship with Marta is totally outside of all this. It takes place in another sphere, on another planet. I'm crazy about her, but in the way that mystics are crazy about God. Marta is my God.

Maybe this is the point.

Can one be jealous of God?

Weren't almost all the mystics jealous of him? Weren't Saint Teresa of Avila, Saint John of the Cross, Saint Ignatius of Loyola jealous of him?

Isn't Marta herself jealous of him, seeing that she does not hesitate to accuse Saint Augustine of having wanted to take possession of him exclusively?

So there: I'm jealous of Marta in the way that Marta is jealous of God.

Whether, in my case, this type of jealousy somehow

involves that which is commonly called "love", I couldn't say, for the simple reason that, on a personal level, I know nothing about this "love". If anything, all I know about it is what I've read and what I see in books and in the newspapers (reading is part of my work, although I prefer to read books which are different than those I have to read). Judging from both everyday reality and literary fiction, it's a type of "love" which leads to nothing but death. The famous line of *The Ballad of Reading Gaol*– "Yet each man kills the thing he loves"[17] –would make one think that Oscar Wilde was stating a kind of ontological principle on the criminal nature of love. "In the end Paulina killed the man she loved" Pierre-Jean Jouve writes in *The Desert World*. "All normal people have at one time or another desired the death of those they love" Camus has Meursault say.

It was after four in the morning when I put the *Loves* back on the book shelf and went back to bed.

Last evening Marta came to the editorial office unexpectedly again, once more entering my office without having herself announced (it had been seven or eight days since we'd seen each other).
"Why don't you come with me to see the Matisse exhibition at the Campidoglio?" she asks, ex abrupto. "I have to write an article for 'Third Millennium'".
"Sure, let's go".

Her elegance is exceptional.
A white suit, white shoes and stockings, a strand of white pearls around her neck.

The Campidoglio is already crawling with people when we get there.
The crowds in the galleries are suffocating.
We can barely get close to the paintings.

From time to time, Marta gets left behind, or I remain behind; there is such a mob that we can't get through.

We meet up again, then drift apart again, in an ever-increasing chaos.

All of a sudden, loud shouting can be heard from one of the galleries.

I go to the spot where all the noise is coming from.

Marta is railing against one of the guests, a man of about thirty.

"You're a sex maniac!" she says to him, trying to slap him.

"You're crazy" he replies, stepping back to avoid the slap.

"You're a contemptible individual!" she persists, trying to kick him.

"You're a schizophrenic" he comes back at her, raising his right arm to strike her.

I block his arm and push him backwards.

A free-for-all breaks out; even the Campidoglio guards get involved.

I take Marta by the hand, we make our way through the crowd with some difficulty, and get out of there.

"I'm sorry, forgive me, but he said some obscene things to me, he was tailing me, he glued himself to me" Marta says when we reach Piazza Ara Coeli.

"Don't worry about it" I tell her, holding her close to me. "You should never visit art shows on their opening day. There are too many people, it's an exhibition of vanity. We can always see the show tomorrow, in peace and quiet".

"I wanted to write the article tomorrow".

"You can write it the day after tomorrow".

Marta hugs me and gives me a kiss.

"Where do you want to go?"
"I don't know, I'm so upset".
"How about the Casina Valadier?"
"Let's pick a quiet place.
"Casina Valadier is more than quiet".

We take a table on the first floor terrace, which overlooks a large part of the city.
Rome is teeming with golden lights.
The pianist plays musical themes for the tourists, taken from soundtracks of Hollywood films of the Thirties and Forties.

"The other night I saw *Casablanca* again on television" Marta says.
"Please, would you ask the pianist to play *As time goes by*" I tell the waiter.
The pianist smiles at us with a gesture of assent and places his hands back on the keyboard.
Marta takes my hand and gives me a tender look, with a smile that moves me.

We order the aperitif offered by the Casina, then accept the waiter's recommendation.

"I've never been here at night, the atmosphere is very romantic" Marta says to me, raising her glass for a toast.
"I'm happy you like it" I reply, toasting her.
"I'm happier than you".

She takes from her purse the notebook in which she writes her poems.
"Did you finish the poem about beauty?"
"Yes, I didn't tell you before because I wanted to surprise you".
"You can read it now if you'd like, before the waiter serves us".

115

She opens the notebook and reads:

Beauty,
Diabolical illusion,
Plumed serpent,
Fatal idol,
I hate you.

Beauty,
Poisonous flower,
Cancerous jewel,
Ephemeral gleam,
I hate you.

Beauty,
Conceited goddess,
Deceptive Muse,
Cruel Fate,
I hate you.

Beauty,
Burning glass,
Diabolical reflection,
Imago mortis,
I hate you.

"Through grass and flowers the evil streak advanced"[18]
says the Poet. But my entire life is an evil streak.
A way of the cross without stations, nor Veronicas.
There are no compassionate cloths for my face,
No Shroud will ever bear its imprint,
Its memory will be lost in an absolute void.
I am a specter outlined in the sand,
Trampled and wounded by every clumsy foot,
Dissolved by even the slightest wave.

Marta looks up from her notebook.

"Very good, I like it very much".

"Do you really mean it?"

"You're as good as Sylvia Plath".

"Please don't make fun of me. I'll never be capable of writing poems like Sylvia Plath. Not even if I died and were reborn three times would I be able to write poems like hers".

"You're too hard on yourself, Marta".

"I haven't even learned the art of dying from Plath. I'm not even capable of killing myself".

"I'm glad you haven't learned it".

"I haven't learned it because I'm not cut out for it".

"You're cut out for poetry".

"I'm not cut out for anything".

She has tears in her eyes...

"The other night I read Emily Dickinson's poetry" she says, suddenly smiling again. "I got the idea from reading *Darkness Visible*, the book in which William Styron tells about the depression he fell into in the mid-Eighties. It's a heartbreaking book. Have you read it?"

"No. It came to the editorial office, but then I lost sight of it and forgot about it".

"I recommend that you read it. Styron cites Dickinson when he says that his dark mood would hit its lowest point after sunset, in the vanishing afterglow of twilight. That light reminded him of the "slant of light"[19] which inspired the idea of death in Dickinson, and gave him the sensation of suffocating obscurity. So I got the urge to read Dickinson's poems".

"Did you like them?"

"First I want to tell you something else about *Darkness Visible.* In the book Styron also talks about the suicide of Jean Seberg and Romain Gary, whom he knew well. The police had found her dead in an abandoned Renault on a street in Paris, and next to the body, which by then was decomposing, was an empty container of barbiturates. It was 1979; she was just 41 years old. Gary killed himself three months later, with a gun shot to the temple. He was 65, and still loved her, although they had been divorced for some time. Styron maintains that it was a 'double suicide'. But I won't even be fortunate enough to have a 'double suicide'".

"You are *a specter outlined in the sand, / Trampled and wounded by every clumsy foot, / Dissolved by even the slightest wave*. All I had to do was hear those lines of yours one time only, to learn them by heart. Isn't that enough for you?"

"I'll end up like Seberg".

She's about to burst into tears again...

So, Marta, did you like Dickinson's poems?" I ask her, caressing her hair.

"In *Darkness Visible*, Styron says that even Albert Camus suffered from depression and thought about suicide".

"But we knew that, Marta, Camus himself says so in the *The Myth of Sisyphus*. Tell me about Dickinson, please".

"After Sappho and Plath, Dickinson is the poet I love the most now. She's subtle, profound, intuitive. She too is always struggling with the 'mortal illness', with the 'irrevocable creature'; she exalts the gifts of Life but also those of Death. What I like most is that she puts Poetry and Love on the same level. But there are some things in her work that are not convincing".

"Such as?"

"Her insistence on the themes of Immortality and Eternity. Her idea of Beauty doesn't convince me either. She establishes a strict relationship between Beauty and Truth, perhaps going back to Plato, but Plato said that Beauty is a reflection of Good, not Truth. I learned them by heart, her lines about Beauty:

Beauty – be not caused – It Is –
Chase it, and it ceases –
Chase it not, and it abides.[20]

"I like the part about Beauty disappearing and appearing, like a mirage, but I don't like that 'It Is'. Beauty 'isn't', it doesn't exist".

"Marta, I'm proud of you" I say, getting up.

"Now I have a small confession to make: I dressed all in white in honor of Dickinson" she tells me, as we head down toward Piazza di Spagna.

"And I'll read Dickinson in honor of you".

Piazza di Spagna is ablaze.

"The Night of the Stars" is underway, the great annual spectacle of fashion designers and top-models. Under the dazzling light of lamps meant for a film set, Claudia Schiffer and Naomi Campbell are descending the staircase of Trinità dei Monti like priestesses of the Temple of Vesta or lionesses of the Circus Maximus.

We watch the last of the show from the window of my attic; then, exhausted, we go to bed and dream about Volos.

AT VOLOS

Marta throws open the window of the room in which we've spent the night, in a hotel at the port, on the third floor.

The room is flooded with light.

It's nine thirty. We just got up.

Beneath her silk dressing gown of transparent pinkish white, her body, nude, appears to be surrounded by precious veiling; it glows like a sculpture beneath its patina.

"Come and see" she says, running her fingers through her hair.

The port is already in full chaos. Boats, dinghies, yachts, hydrofoils, ships crossing in front of one another, crowds of tourists circulating among the kiosks and taverns with garish signs, vendors hawking their merchandise in a loud voice. Beyond the masts of the boats anchored in their moorings, the sea is a pure blue that turns dark green near the line of the horizon; outlines of mountains still shrouded in haze can be seen along the horizon, as far as one – Olympus, perhaps – which blends in with the sky.

"The Argonauts who went in search of the golden fleece set sail from here" Marta tells me with a captivating smile.

She's beautiful. Without makeup, her face reacquires a natural purity, like that of a pearl just found in a seashell. Her lips are like sensuous silk, slightly pale, sweet.

"Marta, I'm very hungry".
"Me too".

The trip had been pleasant but tiring, and as soon as we arrived, around midnight, we had gone straight to bed without having supper.

I order breakfast.

Marta has brought along a "small portable library" in her suitcase, which she now takes out: the *Memoirs* and *Hebdomeros* of Giorgio de Chirico, Alberto Savinio's *Tragedy of Childhood*, Cocteau's *Le mystère laïc*, a guidebook for Greece.

She puts the books on the table near the window, keeping the guidebook in hand.

"In ancient times Volos was called Iolkos" she tells me, leafing through the guidebook, after the waiter has placed the tray on the little table in the right hand corner of the room, and after we have seated ourselves in the two red armchairs beside the wall.

"The inhabitants were known for their workmanship with wood, which they took from the forests of Pelion; they specialized in building boats, which they used to travel to the surrounding islands. Tessaglia is known throughout the world for its "stars of stone", the Meteors, or rather the sandstone spurs which had surfaced from the sea bed. In 1400 the cenobite Athanasius founded the Meteoron, the Great Meteor, on which he had the church of the Transfiguration built".

She closes the guidebook and puts it on the little table.

I take off my pajamas and put on a pair of shorts, leaving my torso bare.

She stays in her dressing gown.

She doesn't know where to put her legs, so she stretches them out on my knees, her bare feet raised; her dressing gown opens. I had never seen her sex so nicely displayed, except that afternoon when she came up to my place under the pretext of wanting to see de Chirico's atelier from the window of my attic.

"Giorgio was born on July 10, on a very hot day" she tells me, as I pour coffee. "He was baptized in the church of the Immaculate Conception. He was still a child when he began to draw and paint. He did his first painting when he was nine years old; it depicted a horse in motion. If we're still here on July 10, we'll celebrate the centenary of his birth in a tavern on the port. We'll dance the *sirtaki*, it will be an event for us. What do you think?"

To tell the truth, I'm thinking about her pubis. I had never seen one so splendid, also because I haven't seen very many of them. Some I remember with horror, like the Brazilian girl's: jet-black, dense, bristly, it looked like a bush of *ruscus aculeatus*; or that of the woman who wanted me to end up like the protagonist in *Realm of the Senses*: it reminded me of the enormous pubis of the woman Courbet painted in the *Origin of the World*.

Marta also has beautiful breasts. They lift up from her chest with force and grace at the same time, in perfect harmony; the aureoles surround the nipples like lace of burnished gold.

"In 1955 Volos was destroyed by an earthquake and was almost entirely rebuilt" Marta says, removing her legs from my knees and getting up to get dressed.

"Probably the church of the Immaculate Conception was destroyed as well, and I don't know if that was rebuilt. We'll have to do some research. We'll go to the Tourist

Bureau right away to get some information. I have to collect as much material as possible, because I want to rewrite my thesis and then find a publisher who will publish it".

While I'm waiting, I pick up two of the books which Marta brought. I sit in one of the two armchairs and leaf through them, stopping on this or that page where they talk about Volos.

Maybe it's because I want to go out and explore the city, or because I want to go dive into the sea where there's a "star of stone", but I find the books deadly boring.

I put them back and pick up the guidebook.

I rest my feet on the edge of the other armchair, light a cigarette and scan the guidebook, occasionally watching the coils of smoke rising in a spiral in the tremulous sunlight.

"I'm ready" Marta says, coming back into the room.

Now I see a double image of her: her real image and the image reflected in the long vertical mirror on the left wall.

A fresh image: she seems taller and more slender, her tapering legs extending from her orange-red shorts, her white tennis shoes, her breasts emerging from her embroidered white blouse, her hair shining in the morning sunlight, rendered even more radiant by a mother-of-pearl barrette.

Before we leave, she puts the books in her bag.

She makes way through the crowd with a quick, light step; the wind rising off the sea seems to give her wings as she walks.

"Here we are, there's the Tourist Bureau" she says, pointing out a sign a short distance away.

She goes in, and pushing through the crowd with little regard, reaches the counter; I follow her, but I'm held back by the people who were there before us.

"You don't know anything!" she shouts at the women standing behind the counter; she makes her way back through the crowd and walks out.

I didn't hear what the woman she had questioned said to her, and there's nothing I can do but go after her.

She walks along uncertainly, seemingly unsure of her destination.

She's like a bird tossed about by the wind.

I catch up with her and take her by the arm.

"Marta, what happened?"

"They don't know anything, whether the church of the Immaculate Conception still exists, not even who Giorgio de Chirico was".

"Don't get upset, Marta, please; we can consult an art historian".

"It's all starting out badly, as I knew it would".

I lead her to a bar.

"Marta, why don't we go and see the Great Meteor?"

"The Great Meteor is a long way from here".

"Then let's go see the Meteors of Kalabamka, even Giorgio de Chirico and his brother used to go there when they were kids".

"I want to know if the church of the Immaculate Conception still exists, or if it's been rebuilt".

"We have plenty of time to find out, Marta. For now let's go to some quiet bay. I read in your guidebook that there are bays all around us where the sea is still the way it was when Homer sang about it".

"We'll go wherever you want, but I have no intention of ever setting foot in that Tourist Bureau again".

I ask a boatman for information. He tells me that there is a secret bay near Kalabamka, but it's difficult to reach. "You have to take the ferry for Kalabamka, get off there, and then continue on foot along a rocky path for at least fifteen minutes".

"But it's worth it" he adds.

We get on board.

We get off at a small pier carved out of the rock and continue on foot.

The bay, hidden behind a high spur which is impervious to the sea, is truly enchanting.

The water is a clear, transparent green.

The pebbles that make up the beach are smooth and shiny, like stones polished by hand.

All around are sunny plains and wild plants; in the background, both to the right and to the left, are mountains which stretch toward the sky; a demolished building can be seen on one of them, perhaps an abandoned monastery.

On the beach, tall, blond young women take a swim in the nude, then stretch out in the sun like naiads.

Marta strips on the pebbles and dives into the water.

She reaches open water with a few strokes; then she disappears and reappears, leaping out of the water like a dolphin; then she is lost in the distance, in the incandescent sea.

A few meters from the beach stands a little white house with blue shutters; it's been built recently: the walls, whitewashed, are still wet.

It's a tavern, run by two young Greeks, tall, dark, and polite.

"We only have Greek salad and beer, plus some mats to spread on the stones, but here you'll regain your health and the joy of living" one of the two young men tells me. He adds: "We're brothers, we come from Los Angeles; back there life has become hell".

I ask for two mats and spread them on the stones.
I look out to sea.
Marta has disappeared.

I strip and dive in as well.
I'd like to go and look for Marta, but I'm not a dolphin like she is.
I swim for a while, then I turn around and float with my back in the water, looking up at the sky.

I have just stretched out on the mat, when a tall, dark girl with long black hair comes out of the water; she lies down on the mat next to mine, on my right.
I ask her if she's seen a woman with tawny hair out at sea.
"Don't worry, she'll come back" she says laughing, as though she were teasing me.
"Is your friend also Italian?" she asks then, still laughing.
I respond yes with a nod of my head.
"Maybe she's playing a game; we're Mediterraneans, full of fantasy" she says.
I ask her where she's from, from what part of Greece, what work she does.
Her name is Atena, she was born in Volos, but her parents took her to New York when she was still a child, and she's now studying Cultural Anthropology at Columbia University there. It's the first time she's been back to Greece. She's in search of her roots, nature in its primitive state, the myth of the Argonauts.
I'd like to tell her that she herself is nature in its primitive state, with her body like a sculpture carved from natural stone, her savage pubis, her man-eating mouth; but I catch a glimpse of tawny hair appearing from time to time among the waves.

Marta comes out of the water.
The *Birth of Venus* comes to mind.

I try to remember the details of that famous painting.

"No, no" I say to myself. "Marta is not resting her feet on a seashell, but on pebbles; she's not hiding her sex with her hair, and her breast with her right hand, but is displaying her body in its entirety; she's not assuming the pose of a goddess, rather she is a living goddess".

"The sea is divine here" Marta says, stretching out on the mat to my left.

"You're divine" I tell her.

"Didn't I tell you she'd come back?" Atena says smiling, before I have a chance to introduce her.

"The 'latin lover' and the Nereid" Marta says with an ironic smile, eyeing her from head to toe.

"This is Atena" I say, gesturing to her; but Marta refrains from greeting her or from turning toward her; instead, she turns the other way.

"They only have Greek salad and beer here" I say to Marta, starting to get up to go to the young Greeks' place.

"I don't want anything".

"Marta, please".

"I want to leave" she says, getting up and putting her clothes back on.

I too get dressed and we walk toward the pier.

We make the trip back in silence.

It's around eight when we get back to the hotel.

"Marta, please, let's change and go have supper in a tavern at the port".

"I don't want to go anywhere".

"Let's go dance the *sirtaki*".

"I hate the *sirtaki*".

"You yourself said you wanted to dance it to celebrate the centenary of the birth of Giorgio de Chirico".

"The *sirtaki* is for a 'latin lover' like you".

"Marta, stop it".

"I should never have come to Volos with you".

"Come on, let's change, Marta. If you don't want to go out, we can eat in the hotel".

"I don't want to eat, I just want to die, to sink into an endless sleep".

She bursts into tears...

She lies down on the bed.

I lie down next to her.

We remain supine, motionless.

A great buzz rises from the port, but we don't hear a thing.

We've lost our sensory faculty.

Time has stopped for us.

"We're two corpses" I think.

From time to time, though continuing to lie supine, I peek at her out of the corner of my eye to see if she's asleep; but she's not sleeping.

From time to time, I stretch slightly to the left, to look at the clock on the bedside table, but it seems to me that the hands are always in the same place.

"Even the clock has lost its sense of time" I say to myself.

I get up on tiptoe, I drink a glass of water, I sit down in one of the two red armchairs beside the wall and light a cigarette.

I don't know what to do; my head feels empty and confused.

I put out the cigarette and go back to bed.

Now she's sleeping, her breathing nearly imperceptible, as though she were in a coma.

I doze; then I too fall into a coma.

I awake around eleven.

Marta isn't there.

I sit up in bed and look around me: there's nothing of hers.

I get up and go into the living room: there's nothing of hers anywhere.

I wash my face and go down to the lobby.

"The lady left early this morning, around six" the concierge tells me. "Our bellboy took her to the port, you can speak with him".

"I carried her suitcase as far as the port, then I came back to the hotel" the bellboy says.

"You didn't see which hydrofoil or boat she left on?"

"No, I don't know if she went to Athens, Salonicco, or someplace else".

I go back up.

I call Alitalia.

"The name Marta Cohen appears on the passenger list for the July 2 flight from Rome to Athens, but she doesn't appear to have departed or reserved a seat for the return to Rome" a woman's voice tells me. "On the other hand, there were no seats and her ticket for the return to Rome was an open one".

I call the other airlines, but the name Marta Cohen does not turn up on any of their flights from Athens to Rome.

I call Alitalia again to make a reservation for my return to Rome, but the same voice as before tells me that the only available seat is on July 5, on the eight o'clock evening flight.

I ask if she can put me on a waiting list, but she tells me that the waiting lists are full. I reserve a seat for July 5.

I go down to the port, have coffee, and take the ferry to Kalabamka.

I reach the secret bay.

Atena isn't there.

I don't see any bathers; the sea is a desert of light.

No naiads, neither in the water nor on the beach.

I don't even see the two brothers who run the tavern.

I go behind the tavern, but there's no one.

A small chapel rises a short distance away; its cross is lop-sided, as though bent by the wind.

I approach.

It's closed, abandoned.

There's a Byzantine fresco on the facade; it appears eaten away by the salty sea air.

I look at it closely.

It was done recently, and damaged so that it would appear old.

Even the chapel was put up recently, but blackened with smoke and other devices. Signs of fresh mortar are notice-able underneath the dark patina.

"*Timeo Danaos et dona ferentes*" I say to myself.

I go back along the rocky path and return to Volos.

As soon as I get off the ferry, I go into the nearest tavern.

I'm as hungry as a bear.

I have barely sat down when some Greeks in costume and several of the customers begin dancing the *sirtaki*.

I get up and walk right out.

"It's a vile dance, Marta was right" I think, reluctantly.

I wander around the port a little, looking for another place where I can satisfy my hunger.

I spot a French restaurant.

The menu is on the door: escargots, entrecote avec champignons, viande à la bourguignonne...

I sit at an outdoor table.

"Two plates of escargots and a bottle of Chablis" I tell the waiter.

"Are you expecting someone?"
"Don't worry about it".

He sets the table for two; then he brings the two plates of escargots and the bottle of Chablis.

I fill two glasses, eat the escargots from one of the two plates and drink half of the bottle of Chablis, always from my own glass.

The waiter starts to take away both the empty plate and the one which is still full:

"We haven't finished yet" I tell him.

He shakes his head.

I order two entrecotes avec champignons, a bottle of Beaujolais and two more glasses.

"Excuse me, sir, but are you expecting someone?" he asks again.

I'd like to tell him that he's a royal pain in the ass, but he's likable so I refrain.

He brings the two entrecotes avec champignons, the bottle of Beaujolais and two more glasses.

I fill the two glasses, I eat one of the two entrecotes and drink half of the bottle of Beaujolais, always from my own glass.

"Do you want two desserts as well?" the waiter asks.

"Excuse me, but you're a real pain in the ass" I tell him, asking for the bill.

I pay and go on my way.

"Say hello to your *copine* for me" he says with a sarcastic smile, shaking his head.

I go back to the hotel drunk.

I ask for a twelve noon wake-up call and go up to our room.

I fall heavily on the bed.

131

At one o'clock the next day I go down to the lobby, leave my suitcase in the luggage room, pay the bill and return to the French restaurant.

"Did you say hello to your *copine* for me?" the waiter from the night before asks.

"Go fuck yourself, but first bring me two plates of escargots and a bottle of Chablis" I tell him.

"I've never had such an eccentric customer before" he says, under his breath.

"Now you've had a new experience" I say.

I eat one of the two plates of escargots, drink half of the bottle of Chablis, and ask for the bill.

It's around three when I get up from the table.

The waiter watches me until I disappear from view.

I return to the hotel and ask the bellboy to accompany me to the port.

"I'll leave you here just where I left the lady" he says, starting to hand me the suitcase.

"Bring it onto the hydrofoil for Athens, please" I tell him.

"Good luck" he says as I embark, with a smile that is ironic but full of kindness.

I go to Alitalia's counter, then sit down in the restaurant where I drink and wait until they call the eight o'clock flight for Rome.

A DESPERATE SEARCH

As soon as I get off the plane, I dial her home number, but I get the answering machine with a greeting that says: "This is Marta Cohen. This is a recording. I'm not in Rome. I will return to the city at the end of July". I dial her cell phone number, but an anonymous voice answers saying: "The person you are calling is currently unavailable. Please try again later".

At home, I try again: ditto.

As soon as I wake up, around ten o'clock on July 6, I try her numbers once more, but again I hear only her recorded voice on the answering machine and the anonymous voice which repeats: "The person you are calling..."

I get dressed and go over to Via dei Greci 75.

"I haven't seen Ms. Cohen for about a week", the caretaker tells me; she's an elderly, ageless woman, perhaps a contemporary of the cardinal who lived in the building in the seventeenth century. "I'm sorry, I can't tell you anything" she adds with a gentle smile, showing a glimpse of missing teeth.

"Please, if you should see her, call me" I say, giving her my business card.

"I will, don't worry. I don't see well anymore, but I'll have my little granddaughter read me your phone number" she says, putting the card in her pocket.

I go to Caffè Greco.

The women who are on duty in the entry hall as well as the waiters tell me that they often saw her at breakfast time, but that they haven't seen her for several days.

"We miss her, she's so beautiful" one of the waiters murmurs.

In the afternoon, although I know she's on vacation leave, I go to the gallery where she works.

"The last time we saw her was June 30, when she said goodbye before going on vacation" the manager tells me.

I take a walk around the *centro*, along the streets she would usually take, then I return home.

From eight until nine-thirty that evening I call her numbers every ten or fifteen minutes, until I get tired of hearing those monotonous recorded voices.

"I'll try waiting for her at her front door" I say to myself.

I go down around eleven, buy a couple of papers from the newsstand on Piazza di Spagna, and go to the restaurant that stands almost in front of the building in which she lives: it's a few meters beyond, toward Via del Corso, at no. 96.

I sit at an outdoor table and have supper, leafing through the papers from time to time.

They are still full of sexy-gate and the new ecclesiastical scandal. They give more and more provocative details about the first, and for the latter report that the archbishop of Naples, Cardinal Michele Giordano, may be involved in a ring of usurers who demanded interest at a thousand percent.

I linger at the restaurant until two in the morning, when the waiters throw me out so they can close up.

I begin walking back and forth, about fifty meters in

each direction, never losing sight of the door marked with the number 75.

I go on like this until three in the morning, before I admit defeat.

I'd like to go around to the discotheques, but I'm tired and irritated.
"Maybe she hasn't come back to Rome yet" I think, as I go back home.
"But it's an absurd hypothesis" I then tell myself.

The following day I wake up with a brilliant idea.
"I don't know why I didn't think of it before" I tell myself, sitting up in bed.
I pick up the phone and call her parents.
"We don't know anything about her, we haven't seen her for a long time" a male voice, perhaps that of her father, tells me in an unaccented tone.

I sit and think for a while; then I get up, shave, make coffee, put on a pair of shorts and a tee-shirt, and go down to Piazza di Spagna.

"A change of air" I tell myself, as I start up the car which was parked along the incline of San Sebastianello.

I go to the shore, to Fregene, to the famous bathing establishment-restaurant, Mastino's; Federico Fellini had set his first film, *The White Sheik*, there at a time when the place was still a fisherman's shack.

More than with the reflections of sun and sea, the beach is radiant with the dazzling bodies of young people in topless or tanga, their mouths, nipples and navels pierced.

I dive in and swim out to open water; later on I have lunch near the beach, surrounded by those burning bodies. I remain in ecstasy on a lounge-chair until a fiery sunset descends upon the sea, among seagulls rising up in flight.

At ten that night I return to Rome.

Toward midnight I begin to make the rounds of the disco-theques.

I take a quick look at the dance floor and gaze around me, searching for familiar faces. I talk to the disk-jockey and the bouncers.

Nothing.

No one has seen her.

The next day I go to see Sandro Spigai.

"He's the only one who may know something about her" I say to myself as I pass through the gate of his studio apartment on Via Margutta.

Sandro is painting.

On the easel is a canvas depicting a fallen angel.

"You're a terrible friend" he says "I haven't heard from you in over six months".

"You're right, Sandro, I'm sorry".

"Since you met Marta Cohen".

"Do you see Marta, do you know where she is?"

"You're asking me? The last time she came to see me was about two months ago. I had heard strange things about her".

"What things?"

"My secretary had told me that Marta was spending time with a Sicilian writer who had formed a *tìaso* in her home in Rome, or rather an association of young women dedicated to the cult of Aphrodite, lesbian love and poetry. They had discovered the underground neo-Pythagorean basilica that stands near Porta Maggiore and went there

136

once a week. They were fascinated by the sanctuary of Artemis, the Greek sister of Diana, Roman goddess of the hunt".

"But what did Marta tell you?"

"After my discreet questions – hints rather than questions – she admitted to being part of that association and going with her girl friends to the underground neo-Pythagorean basilica at Porta Maggiore. She told me that sometimes she even went there by herself. I then asked her what she found so interesting there, and she said: 'I'm fascinated by the figure of Sappho who hurls herself into the sea from the cliff of Leucas with a cupid'. She added: 'I hope to be able to resolve my problems'. 'But how?' I asked her. 'I'd like to free myself' she replied 'from all earthly passion to attain total purity of the soul, absolute completeness of Being. Maybe you don't know this, but the figure of Sappho portrayed in the basilica of Porta Maggiore represents the image of the soul, and the poetess' dive into the water symbolizes the liberation of the body from the heavy weight of matter'".

"What else did she tell you?"

"That she was thinking about going to India. She wanted to go to Dharamsala, in Northern India, to meet with the Dalai Lama... I had never seen her so distant before, so enigmatic, so confused... She was about to leave, but then she turned back and said to me: 'I brought you the last issue of "Third Millennium", there's an article of mine on the Poussin exhibit at the Palazzo delle Esposizioni in Rome. I hope you find time to read it. I'd like to know what you think of it'. 'I can read it right away' I told her, taking the magazine from her hands".

"She sat down again".

"It was a very beautiful article. She had fallen in love with Poussin's blue. To explain that blue she had gone back to the one hundred and twenty variations of blue that are admired in the mosaics of the Blue Mosque in Istanbul and

137

to the blues of Ravenna in the mosaics of Sant'Apollinare in Classe... I gave her my compliments, but she brushed them off saying: 'I've known Poussin since I was a girl. I had seen him many times at the Louvre. He's fascinated me ever since then'... Then her mood changed and she said: 'Sandro, I don't know what to do with myself'. I remember saying to her: 'Marta, your writing is magical. You should write more and spend less time in that gallery'. 'But how?' she asked. 'Write, keep writing, sooner or later they'll become aware of your talent' I replied; but she was rather skeptical. She left a great sadness inside me".

"Her articles are extraordinary, but the trouble is she hasn't got the least bit of faith in herself, Sandro".

"Are you still seeing her?"

"We went to Greece together, to Volos, the town where Giorgio de Chirico was born, but she disappeared during the trip, and now I don't know where she is".

"Maybe she's in India".

"Thank you, Sandro" I say, promising to go and see him more often.

FATA VIAM INVENIENT

On July 8, I find a letter in the mailbox. It shocks me: the handwriting on the white envelope is Marta's. I put it in my pocket and go to Caffè Greco. I take a table out the back, in the second room, which is not as full as the others. I order coffee. I wait for the waiter to bring it. I drink it slowly, then I open the envelope, with trembling hands.

Inside are five double-sided pages, hand written, with large, irregular letters sloping from left to right.

I begin to read:

Dear Andrea,

I am writing you this letter with tears in my eyes. I've suffered a great deal writing it, and I've had to make a great effort. I did it in the hope that you would finally understand me, understand my state of mind, my depression, my anguish. I wanted to tell you that our relationship has no place to go, no way out, as though there were a wall between us. A black wall. The reason is very simple: you don't love me, or I don't feel that you love me, which is the same thing. This is what makes me insecure, troubled, unstable...

I order another coffee, wait for the waiter to bring it, then go back to reading:

I've told you a number of times that I have never been loved by anyone. Well, I don't feel loved by you either. Since our earliest times together I've asked you to tell me what you want from me, but you've never given me a clear, reassuring answer. This is because you yourself, deep inside, don't feel that you love me. But now I've understood what you want from me. You want me not to end my life. You could tell me that this is love, but it isn't love; it's egotism, of the worst kind. To put it more clearly, you would like to prove to yourself that you are able to do something that no one else could do: stop me from committing suicide, save me (such an ugly word "save", I hate it with all my heart)...

I order a third coffee, take another break, then bend my head once again over the pages:

Andrea, think about yourself, please. You're ill. You're ill with a sickness that has something demonic about it. Only someone affected by megalomania could conceive of the idea of saving someone else. You know that I've been treated by various psychiatrists in the past, that I underwent analysis. But no one has been able to help me. As your beloved Artaud says, there is no cure for life. The psychiatrists stuffed me with anti psychotic drugs, the psychoanalysts didn't understand me and had more problems than I did. Many of them suffer from the same illness that you do, a sickness which neither they nor you are fully aware of. It's a kind of delirium of omnipotence. But your delirium is worse than theirs, because it's a mystical kind, not scientific or pseudo-scientific. Is it possible that you still haven't understood that I don't want to be saved, but rather loved? That the psychiatrists and psychoanalysts haven't understood it is more than understandable; but that you haven't understood it is horrifying. Andrea, I don't like telling you this, but you have to treat yourself, save yourself...

I pause again; there are still four pages left.
The seventh says:

140

Andrea, you belong to that category of individuals, like psychiatrists and psychoanalysts, who presume to go against destiny. They can't understand that each of us obeys a kind of predetermined fate. Our destiny is already written before we are born, we cannot avoid it, no one has the power to halt its fulfillment. In my case, personally, I am more than certain that my destiny was already written for me. I don't want to repeat things that you already know, but being conceived, born, and raised without love is a misfortune which no one can remedy.

To conclude: it's useless for us to continue to look for one other, to see each other, to deceive and wound each other reciprocally. It doesn't make any sense. I won't look for you anymore. You shouldn't look for me anymore. I implore you, Andrea, forget me.

At this point, after the signature, there's a P.S.
It says:
"I'm sending you my latest poem".
The poem fills the following two pages; the last one is almost blank.
I read the poem as well:

Dying
Is an art, like everything else.
I do it exceptionally well,
Wrote Sylvia Plath. But for me dying
Is not an art, nor a skill,
The awesome skill of dying.
For me dying is a nightmare.
Every most intimate fiber of mine
Trembles at the thought
Of the "irrevocable creature".
"Sister Death", "Sweet Death"
Are a hallucination of saints in ecstasy,
Of martyrs on the scaffold.

Death is obscene, an indecent event.
But no one can decline
The mysterious ascent
To the Mount of Olives.
Fata trahunt, Fata viam invenient
Virgil sang.
What must happen
Will happen.
What has been written
Will come to pass.

I slip the pages back in the envelope, put the envelope back in my pocket, and go out.

I wander around a little at random, lost among the crowds.

Then I go back up to the house, and lie down on the bed, supine, looking at the ceiling, mentally counting the cracks, the big ones and the little ones.

"Maybe it's best that you really forget her, assuming you can" I tell myself after a while.

I recall that three or four years ago I spent the summer at Fregene, where I had rented a small house at Villaggio dei Pescatori, the gilded shanty town near the sea where filmmakers, actors and writers gathered.
I call they agency that handles it.
It's available.
I take it for the remaining days of July.
I pack my suitcase and leave around noon.

"For sure I'll be better off here than in Rome" I say to myself, as I'm about to set foot once again in that house, which stands about fifty meters from the villa which Alberto Moravia had had built there in the Seventies, and in which the writer had spent part of his summers.

Before going in, I take a look around.

Moravia's villa seems more lonely than usual, as though it were abandoned.

"That villa is his portrait" I think, seeing again its drab, square outline looming beside a slow, dirty rivulet; there's a black spiral staircase on the right, and windows edged in rotted green and discolored red, making the house seem even more desolate and sad.

But even the cottage in which I had spent a lovely summer three or four years earlier has changed.

The inside is untouched: at the entrance, there's a small living room with a little dining table and chairs; on the left, a tiny kitchen with a window that looks out on the bed of reeds that borders the stream; on the right a bedroom with a double bed and two armchairs, a shelf for the television set, and a bench with a telephone. The bedroom gets its light from a window that looks out on the garden of the adjoining house.

Everything is white: walls, ceiling, window frames, the little table, chairs, armchairs, shelf, bench, telephone.

There is an air of cleanliness, delicate and pleasing.

But the outside is a disaster. In the small garden in front, a wild plant, grown excessively, extends high above and overruns the entire area: the branches and foliage surpass the roof, while the roots, which look like enormous varicose veins, have penetrated even beneath the foundation, like the coils of a subterranean animal, shaking it and raising it up from the earth.

I have the feeling that the house might collapse any minute now, that it might suddenly fall down around me.

"It's just the right house for me" I say to myself, putting on my bathing suit and going down to the beach.

After the first day, I begin to follow a kind of fixed routine.

During the day at Mastino's, at night at Le diable au corps sur la plage, the summer branch of the galactic discotheque on Via di Propaganda, which toward midnight is besieged by frenzied youths.

Precocious vampiresses, medusas or sorceresses, half naked, glittering, phosphorescent, with mouths of blood-black, violet-black, green-black, heads with anguished manes, tattoos on arms, necks, breasts, and stomachs, pierced noses, tongues, nipples, and navels, bodies sprinkled with silver or carmine dust.

Stuffed with smart drugs and hallucinogenic mushrooms, they copulate unrestrainedly until the small hours, at which time they dive naked into the sea or jump into their boyfriends' cars or on their own motorcycles, spreading terror along the coastal roads, like swarms of bats or rapacious nocturnal birds.

Many of them have strange names: Priscilla, Orchidea, Selvaggia. But even stranger is their mood, so to speak. There's never a night, or a dawn, in which one of them, especially one of those with the most promising mouths, doesn't follow me at my slightest gesture, I in my car, she on her motorcycle, until we reach the bedroom of the precarious little house.

Some of them are little masters of the oral art, others terribly awkward, but they perform so as to appear amoral, maltreating my sex. Sometimes, before going into the house, we dive into the sea naked, under the rising sun. Toward six or seven they get back on their motorcycle and disappear.

But this morning the spell was broken.

I was in bed with one of them when the phone rang around six.

"Who's calling?" I ask.

"San Giacomo hospital" a male nurse replies. "A lady wants to speak to you. I'll put her on".

"It's Marta, please come".

I dismiss my partner and get dressed to go out.

144

At nine I'm at San Giacomo's.

Marta is lying on a bed in the women's ward on the first floor, her wrists bandaged, her face waxen.

"Thank you for coming" she says in a weak voice, smiling tenderly at me.

I sit down beside her, on her left.

"I had them call you because I lost the golden unicorn that you gave me. I'd like you to go to the house and look for it. The keys should be with the caretaker".

"I'll find it".

As I start to get up, a young man approaches her and caresses her hair.

"John Barth" Marta says to me. "He's the one who helped me (she was about to say "saved me", but she swallows her words).

"Pleased to meet you, thank you" I tell him, greeting him with a gesture of the hand.

"It's no thanks to me, it was only by accident that I arrived at the right moment" he replies.

"Nevertheless, thank you" I tell him, and go out.

The bed is full of blood.

Even on the floor, from the bed to the door, there are bloody tracks, a small reddish trail.

The unicorn is under the bed, in a dark corner.

I put it in my pocket and go back down; but before dropping the keys off at the caretaker's, I go to Via della Croce and have duplicates made.

"I was sure you'd find it" Marta says with a tender smile, asking me to please put it in the drawer of her bedside table.

"I hope it protects you".

"It's my talisman. Even Dali used to say that the unicorn brings good luck. Maybe all this happened to me because I lost it".

"Let's hope you don't lose it again" I tell her, saying good-bye and that I hope she gets well soon.

Before leaving the hospital, I go to the Emergency Room.

"Ms. Cohen" one of the doctors on duty tells me, reading from the information on the register, "cut the veins of her wrists on July 20, that is, six days ago. She was brought here by a young man, John Barth, born in London in 1979, a student at the Accademia di Belle Arti on Via Ripetta". He raises his eyes from the register and adds: "At first, her condition appeared very serious, because she had lost a lot of blood. We had to give her a lot of transfusions. But the second day she began showing signs of recovery, and now she's much better".

"When do you anticipate releasing her?" I ask.

"If all goes well, within two weeks".

I return to Fregene, but I go to see her every day until she is released.

THAT DIZZYING PLUNGE INTO THE TIBER

Marta is released on August 7, and on the 10th she goes back to the gallery, although she feels an increasing lack of enthusiasm for her work (besides that, she still has scars on her wrists and is ashamed of them).

I had gone back to the editorial office on August 1, after having escaped the collapse of the little house at Villaggio dei Pescatori.

But since August 7, we've hardly seen each other.

She doesn't come looking for me; I don't go looking for her.

For the most part, we meet by chance.

I ask her how she is, she replies that she's well, and we say goodbye.

We act as though we were mere acquaintances, if not perfect strangers.

To tell the truth, I nearly always look in on the discotheques in the area, in the hope of meeting her casually. She does the same thing more or less, or similar things, even more openly, in fact, more predictably. Beginning on August 7 or 8, both during the day and during the night – more so during the night than during the day – my phones ring continually, but no one speaks. As soon as I say: "Hello, who's there?", whoever's on the other end hangs up. I'm almost certain that it's her, also because it had never happened before, or only rarely, as it does to everyone. By now I've acquired an unusual perception for the ringing of the telephone. If it's Marta calling me, the ring has a kind of special tremor, almost as though imprinted by her state of mind, her neurosis, her anguish.

We look for each other without telling one another, both of us hiding the fact that we're seeking one another, feigning reciprocal indifference.

The other day I wanted to call her to ask her if she wanted to spend the Ferragosto holiday with me; but each time I was about to call her, I thought it over again, until finally I gave up the idea.

We reach the end of August like this, without ever calling each other if you don't count the silent calls and my "Hello, who's there?" which goes unanswered.

"I hope she's found someone who loves her, that she feels loved, and that she's regained her self-assurance" I tell myself from time to time, but without believing it in the least.

The truth is that without her I have the feeling that I'm passing my time in a vacuum, that my days follow one another in a debilitating monotony, that life itself doesn't make sense to me any more, aside from my work; but even my work doesn't seem to make sense any more now, or it doesn't seem to interest me as it did before.

"I'm living in chaos" I often think, remembering having read, in the commentary to *Beauty*, that "chaos" means "vacuum", or rather, a space in which nothing exists.

"Now there's only nothingness for me: the nothingness of monotony, or the monotony of nothingness" I tell myself.

But on September 15 that "vacuum" is suddenly filled again, converting back to chaos, according to the meaning commonly given to this word.

Yet another phone call fills it up, its ringing breaking the silence of my bedroom in the middle of the night.

"Hello, who's there?" I say, thinking that it's Marta and that no one will answer; but a male voice says to me:

"It's John Barth, forgive me for calling you at this hour, but Marta cut her wrists again. She's here, at San Giacomo hospital. Her condition is very serious".

"Thank you, I'll be there right away" I tell him.

I arrive at the hospital in less than ten minutes.

"They're operating on her" John Barth tells me, near the entrance to the women's ward on the first floor. "The doctors on duty in the Emergency Room told me her condition was desperate".

"Let's hope they're able to save her" I say.

We remain there, in silence, smoking one cigarette after another.

Only toward five o'clock does one of the doctors who operated on her come out:

"The operation went fairly well. It was quite difficult, also because it was the second time she slit her wrists and she had lost a lot of blood. She's still under anesthesia. When she wakes up, we can be more specific. The prognosis is guarded".

"When will the anesthesia wear off?" I ask him.

"Within an hour. You can come back around six, or stay here, if you'd like".

Without discussing it, we decide to wait.

Toward six the same doctor tell us:

"She woke up a quarter of an hour ago, and after a while she began to show some slight signs of recovery. The symptoms are encouraging, but we can't reverse the prognosis yet. Come back around ten".

We go out without speaking.

149

At ten o'clock I'm back in the hospital.

"She's out of danger" says John Barth, who is already at the entrance to the first floor ward and has spoken with the nurses.

"Thank God" I say.

"It won't be possible to see her until tomorrow; let's hope she recovers quickly" he says.

He goes away, but I remain there, waiting to speak to one of the doctors who operated on her.

Toward eleven thirty I'm able to speak to one of the doctors making the morning rounds.

"Ms. Cohen is out of danger, that's all I can tell you for now".

I ask him when it will be possible to see her.

"Come back tomorrow morning, or this afternoon".

I too go away.

At six that evening I return to the hospital.

A nurse allows me to go in and see her.

She's asleep...

I sit beside her bed.

After a while, she wakes up. She looks at the bottle containing the intravenous solution. She moves her head slightly, and attempts a half smile.

"She's a strange woman: fragile yet very strong" the doctor making the afternoon rounds tells me. "None of us thought she would recover this quickly".

I want to ask him how long her hospitalization will last, but it would be too premature a question.

At seven John Barth arrives.

I say goodbye to her, wishing her a quick recovery.

Before leaving the ward, I turn and give her another wave.

She smiles at me.

150

In the days that follow John Barth and I continue to take turns at her bedside, until she is released at the beginning of October.

During all this time I never once saw her parents, nor had I seen them during her last stay in the hospital; maybe they don't even know that she slit her wrists two times.

Upon the advice of her doctors, Marta has had to stay home since the beginning of October, to rest and regain her peace of mind. I go to see her every day, bringing her what she needs and also some little gifts. She never fails to thank me, telling me insistently that I'm very kind; and she arranges it so that I don't run into John Barth in her apartment. From time to time, though without saying so explicitly, she makes me understand that it is my fault that she cut her wrists two times; but I ignore her hints, pretending I didn't get them. I have no intention of starting all over again, nor, on the other hand, do I intend to subject her to stressful discussions. During the time we spend together, usually an hour a day, I take great care to avoid thorny subjects, speaking instead about trite, ordinary matters, entirely removed from our problems.
But she gets impatient with me.
"You're evading" she says to me.
"I'd like to evade forever, but I can't, maybe I'll never be able to" I answer, mentally.

At the beginning of November, Marta goes back to the gallery, and we start meeting again. We see each other almost every day, except for those days when she has a work engagement, or so she tells me (on those days, she sees John Barth; I'm sure of it, because previously she was never so evasive about telling me that she had a work engagement, or else she would tell me what the engagement was and ask me to go with her), or when she prefers

151

to go to the movies with her girlfriends, again according to what she tells me.

As much as I avoid touching on delicate subjects, she always finds a way to involve me in her problems.

Sooner or later, she brings the discussion back to the same subject, which is like an obsession with her: it's my fault that she slit her wrists two times.

I want to tell her that she's right, at least in part: I don't love her as she would like me to, or I don't do everything possible to make her feel loved by me.

But I refrain from telling her so.

"It's best that I don't tell her, for a lot of reasons" I think. "First because it's only partly true, and also because it would lead her to think that she has found the cause of her depression, which would probably aggravate her situation. It's not as though she enjoyed exceptional mental health before we met each other at Sandro Spigai's studio. She was visibly restless, neurotic, unpredictable. Anyone can see that her problems go back to a remote time, to the prenatal period even, when she was still in her mother's womb. Maybe even then she was aware that her parents had conceived her without love. She's well aware of it, more than I, more than anyone else.

Our arguments drag on, more and more listlessly, with an obsessive, exasperating repetition.

And so we come to the night when I began this story, the night she tries to kill herself with poison.

It's the night between January 20 and 21, her birthday.

To mark the occasion, she gives herself a nice bottle of barbiturates.

After her third attempt at suicide, Marta provokes me to an extreme: she lies to me more and more, flirts with men in my presence, and walks out on me suddenly in cafes or restaurants, both day and night. She consistently dumps me when we're in crowded or socially prominent places such as the famous cafes of Piazza del Popolo or Piazza Navona. When she ditches me at night, she continually changes direction, to make me lose track of her.

I invite her to go to the movies or theatre, hoping she won't walk out on me there as well, but she says there's nothing interesting to see.

"I saw Rosi's *La tregua*, Mihaileanu's *Train de vie* and Benigni's *La vita è bella*: one more depressing than the other" she told me a few nights ago. "It's obscene to use the Holocaust to try to make people laugh".

The other night Marta wanted to go to the Paradise, one of her favorite places, where we were to have celebrated her birthday. It stands on the Tiber, near the Sant'Angelo bridge; from the terrace a metal staircase leads down to the gravel river bank, to a small teetering dock where rowboats and other boats are pitching about, waiting for whoever may want to admire Rome from below, despite the rankness of the water.

We ate and drank; she was happy, sensual, seductive.

Then we went to the bar on the terrace, where we drank some more.

The alcohol made her even more euphoric, more exciting.

"This is my birthday party" she told me suddenly, pressing me to her and kissing me sensuously.

I wanted to take here right there.

But all of a sudden she goes to the metal staircase and runs down it, at the risk of slipping on her high heels at any moment and falling into the water below.

I catch up with her while she is on the small wobbly

dock: she takes hold of me and tries to drag me with her into the river, but I grab her in turn, I turn her around, and push her back up the staircase. She twists away, evades me, tries to go down again, falls, gets back up, falls again, until I overtake her and carry her bodily back up to the bar.

She orders another whisky and drinks it happily, laughing.

"Maybe she's convinced that I'm ready to do anything for her, no matter how crazy it is" I think.

The reason she's provoking me ever more insanely seems clear: now she can no longer deny, neither to herself nor to me, that it was I who "saved" her.

If I had not gone up to her apartment that night between January 20 and 21, as though obeying an obscure premonition, she would almost certainly have died.

This is what incites her madness.

The night before last she called me at three in the morning.

"I'm going to jump out the window" she screams.

"I'll be right there".

She leaves the phone off the hook.

She appears to be crying; then her voice becomes weaker; then there are other indistinct sounds; finally nothing.

I go down quickly.

I don't want to find her crushed on the pavement.

The idea flashes through my mind that she's waiting for me to arrive so she can plunge down on top of me, or make me witness her end.

But it would be too prosaic a death for an emulator of Sappho.

Via dei Greci is more deserted than ever.

The old man with the deformed face and the eyes of a mole is not around. Maybe he's sick, or maybe dead.

The trash bin looms in the corner like a small, abandoned throne.

When I reach the seventh floor, the door is open.

I expected to find her undone, her eyes red from crying, her face overwhelmed by anguish; instead she is beautiful and glowing, her red dressing gown covering her naked body.

"I needed to be with you" she says.

"And I with you" I say, but she doesn't catch my irony, or pretends not to get it.

"Come on" she says, with a knowing smile, leading me into the bedroom.

She slips off her dressing gown and sprays on a new perfume, so strong it makes me dizzy.

She takes a pillow from the closet, puts it on the carpet near the bed, on the right side, kneels on it and bends her head over me…

She demonstrates the virtuosity of a geisha.

"Don't you want to sleep with me?" she asks, after we are free of every trace of sex.

"Of course, what a question!" I reply, getting into her bed.

She lies down at my side, and falls asleep.

She smiles in her sleep.

"Now she thinks she can do whatever she wants with me" I say to myself, leaving her apartment around ten (she has already gone).

And yet, if I had told her: "Go ahead, jump out the window!" maybe she would have jumped.

She would have had proof that she had lost her desperate battle with me, and might have ended her life.

Last night I called her to ask if she wanted to have supper with me, or go to the movies; she told me she had a work engagement, excusing herself repeatedly.

I had supper alone; then, around midnight, I went to the Paradise.

Marta is there; she's at the bar on the terrace, with John Barth.

They're standing at the bar; they have a bottle of whisky in front of them. She's drunk.

I too go to the bar.

"Would you like a whisky?" John Barth asks.

"Get lost, you idiot! What are you waiting for, you ugly shit?" Marta orders him.

John Barth goes away.

"My savior has arrived!" Marta says, with an ironic smile.

The waiter laughs, amused.

"He's more miraculous than Jesus Christ!" she adds, with a sarcastic laugh.

"Marta, please" I say, moving toward her.

"Get thee back, Satan!" she says, drawing back.

"Come on, come and save me one more time!" she shouts, moving in a dance step toward the metal stairway.

I make to move toward her again, but she reaches it with a leap, descending it headlong.

I remain at the bar, sitting down and ordering a whisky.

After a while she returns.

She approaches me, smiling a radiant smile.

She's redone her makeup, combed her hair, put on perfume.

She's more beautiful than ever in the moonlight, with a mysterious kind of beauty.

"I've never seen you so radiant, Marta".

She kisses me.

"You're divine".

She kisses me again.

"I love you, Marta".

She kisses me a third time, saying: "I know you love me, Andrea. You're an angel, but I'm an impossible woman. I wish I were different, you know that. If you can be patient for a little while longer, sooner or later I will be, and we'll be happy together".

"I'm sure of it, Marta".

"Come" she says gently, taking me by the hand.

She leads me to a place in darkness, open to the river.

"The view is very romantic here" she says. "Look how beautiful Castel Sant'Angelo is in the moonlight!"

"It's stupendous, Marta".

"It's more evocative than Notre Dame seen at night from the banks of the Seine".

"It seems like a mirage, Marta".

"I'd like to go with you to see Notre Dame from the banks of the Seine some moonlit night".

"We'll go, Marta".

She draws me close to her and begins to kiss me, tenderly.

She kisses my hands…

She kisses my face…

She kisses my mouth…

She pulls me closer to her.

I free myself from her grip and push her into the river.

She falls in with a dull thud.

She reemerges from the current, waving her hands…

Then she disappears, swallowed up by the whirlpools.

Notes

[1] Unless otherwise credited, translations of cited works are attributable to the current translator.

[2] Translated by Justin O'Brien.

[3] Translated by Mary Barnard.

[4] English translation provided by Costanzo Costantini.

[5] Sylvia Plath, "Lady Lazarus" in The Collected Poems, Harper, 1992.

[6] The slight difference in spelling refers to the Italian "caso" (chance) and "caos" (chaos).

[7] Original text provided by Costanzo Costantini.

[8] Frazer, The Golden Bough, Penguin Books edition, 1996.

[9] Original text provided by Costanzo Costantini.

[10] Translated by W.H.D. Rouse.

[11] Ibid.

[12] Ibid.

[13] Translated by Peter Green.

[14] Ibid.

[15] Ibid.

[16] Ibid.

[17] Online text of Oscar Wilde's poem.

[18] Dante, Purg., VIII:100. Translated by Allen Mandelbaum.

[19] Cited by William Styron in Darkness Visible, Random House, 1990, p. 45.

[20] Emily Dickinson, The Complete Poems, Little, Brown, 1960.

INDEX

THE MYTH OF SISYPHUS	5
AN *AMOUR FOU*	15
THE TEMPLE OF THE SUN	24
PURE VERTIGO	30
DIANA, THE TEENAGER WITH THE HEAD OF *GRUS CINERINA*	39
NO ONE WILL EVER LOVE ME	45
THE END OF THE WORLD IS NEAR	51
"DIANA'S MIRROR " AT NEMI	61
FAMILY, I HATE YOU	72
THE ENIGMA OF THE DEATH WISH	80
THE MYSTERY OF THE FEMALE MOUTH	87
BEAUTY IS A DIABOLICAL ILLUSION	96
THE JAPANESE WOMAN WITH A MOUTH OF RUBY RED	102
NEC SINE TE NEC TECUM VIVERE POSSUM	110
AT VOLOS	120
A DESPERATE SEARCH	133
FATA VIAM INVENIENT	139
THAT DIZZYING PLUNGE INTO THE TIBER	147

ITALIAN WRITERS SERIES

Sandro Mayer
Love Letter
The Heartwarming Tale of an Incredible Bond

This seems to be just an ordinary little tale at first, but it leaves the reader overwhelmed with emotion, doubts, speculation, and raises the question: can such a strong bond really exist between a man and a dog? Mayer persuades us that it can. Love Letter *is the extraordinary story of a man, whose initial indifference towards animals is won over by a small poodle called Kalé, who gradually turns his life around, and even helps him discover real faith along the way. The author writes in a concise, down to earth manner, directly addressing and paying homage to the little dog who is no longer with him. He draws us into the story, which unfolds before us like a movie – a thriller, making us laugh and then, moving us to tears. Just like real life.*

Having graduated in Politics, SANDRO MAYER pursued a long career as a special correspondent. He then took on the role of editor of several best selling magazines and women's periodicals, before finally becoming editor of *Gente*, the best selling magazine in Italy. Television is his pastime: he has appeared on many television programs and, as part of the extremely popular *Buona Domenica* show which goes on the air every Sunday, he has hosted a slot in which he has interviewed famous guests and their families. *Love Letter* is his début literary work.

pages 96 • US$ 12.95 / £ 8.95